A YOUNG LION

Dangleboots

Andy sat on his bed examining the dangleboots. Was Dad back and Andy the hat-trick hero because of those nondescript little plastic objects? It couldn't be. Now Andy looked at them carefully, he was disappointed. Mass-produced rubbish.

And they weren't even new. Scuffed; white stripes fading – 80p down the drain. He'd been rooked.

And yet. How else could what he wanted just happen? The dangleboots were the only new element in his life. They *must* be the reason. So. If they worked once, they could work again. He drew in his breath with contentment – he had a secret weapon.

Other Young Lions Storybooks

Floella Hits the Roof *Jane Holiday*
Josie Smith *Magdalen Nabb*
Josie Smith at School *Magdalen Nabb*
Josie Smith at the Seaside *Magdalen Nabb*
Lucy and the Big Bad Wolf *Ann Jungman*
Lucy and the Wolf in Sheep's Clothing *Ann Jungman*
Lucy Keeps the Wolf from the Door *Ann Jungman*
Kim Kong *Lee Pressman*
The Tractor Princess *Kathy Still*
Stuart Little *E. B. White*

A YOUNG LION STORYBOOK

DENNIS HAMLEY

Dangleboots

Illustrated by Tony Ross

Young Lions
An Imprint of HarperCollins*Publishers*

First published in Great Britain by André Deutsch Ltd in 1987
First published in Young Lions 1989
Fourth impression April 1992

Young Lions is an imprint of
HarperCollins Children's Books,
a division of HarperCollins Publishers Ltd,
77–85 Fulham Palace Road,
Hammersmith, London W6 8JB

Dangleboots and the Day After Tomorrow was first
published in *The Methuen Book of Sinister Stories*
(edited by Jean Russell) by Methuen in 1982

Printed and bound in Great Britain by
HarperCollins Manufacturing, Glasgow

Dangleboots and the day after tomorrow

Andy Matthews — known on the football field to everybody as Dangleboots — sat miserably in the front seat of his mother's old Mini. The pair of miniature football boots he had slung over the rear view mirror dangled in front of his face as the little car bucketed along in the teeming rain.

He cast a sideways look at his mother, who sat grim-faced, staring straight ahead and sometimes making the Mini jump like a rabbit being given an electric shock as she made a rough gear-change. Perhaps, thought Andy, if I slipped those dangleboots off the mirror and put them in my pocket she might not be so mad at me.

No, why should I? I bought them. If she doesn't like them it's hard luck. He watched them sway in front of his eyes; the tiny black boots with the white stripes across the instep; just like his own, now wet and muddy inside his sports bag in the boot. Dangleboots on the mirror; dangleboots in the bag. 'Don't give it to Dangleboots.' The cry from his team mates still sounded in his ears.

Why am I so fed up? I should be over the moon. I'm playing on Saturday. I'm in the team at last. But them at school have ruined it and she's ruined it. He hugged his filthy knees and stared again at the tiny boots, remembering.

It wasn't raining when they'd started playing today. Mr Conway had picked two teams so that he could choose the Costers Park School side for Saturday morning's match against their furious rivals Cranbourne Road School. At the start of the game, Andy had no hope. He wanted to be a striker above all things. His heroes were Gary Lineker, Kerry Dixon, Ian Rush. He huffed and puffed, hooked hopefully at every ball that came near him, sending them over the bar, past the post, never in the net. No wonder they called him Dangleboots.

Keep hitting them and the goals will come. That's what his father used to say before he walked out on Andy and his mother. So he kept hitting them. But the goals never came.

'Don't try so hard,' Mr Conway kept calling at him. 'Relax, Andy.'

It wasn't in Andy's nature. 'Sorry, sir,' he said.

'No need to be sorry at me,' said Mr Conway. 'You'll have to slow down. How can I put you in the team when Johnny Caistor's around?'

There was no answer to that. Johnny Caistor really was a striker. He was deadly. Yet at home, practising on the concrete outside the lock-up garages, Andy was great. He *knew* he was. Any angle, any distance — he could hammer them in till the clash of the ball on the steel up-and-over doors brought angry car-owners out to clear him off. He *could* be as good as Johnny Caistor.

But not this afternoon. By half-time, Andy's side was three goals down. Johnny Caistor, with, even at eleven, that lazy elegance only the great players have, had scored all three — while Andy was red-faced, out of breath and scoreless. The half-time break was miserable.

'You're hopeless, Dangleboots.'

'We could have had three ourselves but for you.'

'Let's put him on the wing. He can't do any harm there.'

'I'm the striker,' said Andy doggedly.

'Oh, let him stay there if it means so much to him.'

Mr Conway ran over to them.

'Cool it, all of you,' he said. 'Matthews, you're at it again. Just *think* before you blast away.'

Then the rain came streaking down. Mr Conway ran to the middle and blew his whistle, ignoring the shouts of 'Have a heart, sir.' The second half started. It was worse than the first. Andy's side was penned in the penalty area. Johnny Caistor scored two more; the rain got harder.

'Blow the whistle, sir,' called somebody. 'Put us out of our misery.'

Johnny Caistor was in the middle again; he had made himself space in that instinctive way which marked him out from the rest and was just about to turn and shoot.

'Here comes his sixth.'

No, thought Andy. It won't be. I'll do something right this afternoon. Was what happened next because the pitch was so slippery? Did Johnny Caistor for once lose balance as he turned? Was Dangleboots trying too hard again? Johnny turned just as Andy arrived and the two cannoned into each other and fell — Andy on top, Johnny Caistor sprawled awkwardly underneath. Mr Conway bustled up. Andy rose to his feet.

'I didn't mean it,' he said.

'I can see that, Matthews.'

A sudden shriek of pain came from Johnny Caistor. 'I've bust my leg. You clumsy great pillock, Dangleboots.'

'I doubt you've broken it,' said Mr Conway. 'But it's a nasty sprain.'

Johnny Caistor's ankle was swelling fast. Mr Conway helped him off.

'Great berk. That's the only way you could get in a team, by fouling the best player.'

'I didn't foul him,' protested Andy. 'Mr Conway said it was an accident.'

'What does he know? It was a rotten foul. I'd have sent you off.'

'I didn't mean it,' cried Andy in anguish.

Mr Conway returned alone. 'How is he, sir?' everyone shouted.

'It's only a sprain. The Head's taking him to the doctor. But he won't be playing on Saturday.'

Everyone groaned.

'Matthews plays in his place.'

Howls of disgust rent the air at Mr Conway's words. 'Not Dangleboots, he's useless.'

'I'm not mucking a settled team around,' said Mr Conway. 'Matthews slots straight into Caistor's place.'

'But, sir . . .'

'That's enough,' said Mr Conway. 'Cometh the hour, cometh the man. We'll call it a day for this afternoon.'

On his own, Andy felt cold and wet. And his mother arriving in the old red Mini to take him straight home didn't cheer him up. And she wasn't a bit pleased at his news. 'So that's two lots of dirty football kit I've got to wash. You can't leave me alone even at the weekend.'

He'd really set her going now. He knew it so well he could mime to it. 'Football, football — I wish they'd never invented it. You'll go the same way as your father. That's all he could think of. And look where he is now.'

Actually, Andy had no idea where he was now. But he did remember how they used to play outside the lock-up garages, his father shouting, 'Keep hitting them and the goals will come.' Andy wished he'd come back. Then perhaps his mother would be the happy person he used to know.

So the Mini jolted on through the puddles back to the little house. And the dangleboots swayed to and fro, in front of Andy's eyes.

He had bought the dangleboots the week before on the market, at a little stall he had never noticed previously, run by a man with tanned, leathery skin and a woman with long black hair and dark eyes. The stall was full of odd little knick-knacks, charms, lucky rabbits' feet, Joan the Wads and Cornish piskies. And hanging from a nail on the front of the stall were the boots. Andy had seen boots like them hundreds of times, hanging inside car windows or attached to people's key-rings. He had once or twice thought of buying some but he didn't think his mother would welcome them in the Mini. And anyway, there weren't so many around now. Had they gone out of fashion?

'Like 'em, then, sonny?' said the man with the leathery skin.

'They're all right,' said Andy.

'What would you say if I told you they'd bring you luck? What would you say if I told you they'd make

things happen for you?'

'Not a lot,' said Andy.

'What would you say if I told you those boots were quite unique? What if I told you they were made out of leather from the very ball England won the World Cup with in 1966?'

'I wouldn't believe you,' said Andy.

'And you'd be right not to,' said the man. 'I can see it's a hard task to pull the wool over your eyes.'

Andy turned to move on. But the man kept talking. 'No, the truth about these boots is much stranger than that. It's a terrible, terrifying truth. You've heard of shrunken heads?' he said, leaning forward and speaking in a conspiratorial voice.

'No,' said Andy.

'Well then, you're going to learn something. Years ago, out in the jungle when the cannibal tribes used to go to war, they would eat their enemies to get their strength. And they shrank their heads, to bring them luck and ward off evil spirits.'

'What's that got to do with it?' said Andy.

The man pointed to the little boots. His voice sank to a hoarse but carrying whisper. '*These are shrunken boots*,' he said.

Andy laughed. 'Oh come on,' he said. 'You're having me on.'

'Strike me dead if a word of untruth passes my lips today,' said the man.

'All right, then,' said Andy. 'How do you mean, shrunken?'

'When a really great footballer dies, he leaves his feet to the nation,' said the man.

'You what?' said Andy.

'People give hearts and kidneys. Why shouldn't footballers give feet?'

'But they wouldn't be any good,' said Andy.

'Not to most people, I grant you. But to those like me and my wife they are like gold. Because we shrink the feet and make little boots specially to fit them. And when people buy boots from us, they buy all the magic in the feet of the old player they were made to fit. All the luck and all the talent they used to have passes to the new owner.'

The man's eyes were big and deep and fixed Andy with a stare that made him feel uncomfortable. 'So the little boots make things happen.'

Suddenly, Andy felt scared. He turned to go away. But he was held back by peals of laughter from the man and his wife. 'Don't go away; sonny,' said the man. 'You were a good sport to listen.'

He had taken the boots off the nail. 'Here you are,' he said. 'To you, 80p. And may they bring you all the luck in the world.'

So back home he had brought them. And when he looped them over the rear-view mirror, his mother had said, 'I hope you don't think those things are going to stay there for ever,' but hadn't told him to take them away.

And until that afternoon he had really forgotten about them. Now as he looked at them he recalled the market man's words. All that about the shrunken feet was a load of cobblers. What could a little pair of boots do to make things happen for you? Then he caught his breath. Something *had* happened.

If he had not bought those boots, would he be in Saturday's team?

A nearly sleepless night did not answer the question for him.

The next two days were very unpleasant. Mr Conway

had not changed his mind. Andy was in the team. He had to suffer a lot from everybody. His new team mates were sure he had fouled Johnny Caistor deliberately. At home it was just as bad. His mother was still cross about the extra washing which she seemed to connect with her absent husband.

'Not only did that weak-kneed twerp get out the moment he could but you look like going the same way. Well, I wash my hands of it. I can't seem to influence you.'

So Friday night came with Andy going to bed in a bad state. He put the boots beside him on the pillow and closed his eyes. He remembered his father playing with him outside the garages. 'Keep hitting them and the goals will come.' I wish you were back, Dad, he said to himself. And then he thought about the next morning and his stomach turned.

If only, he thought. If only I could wake up the day after tomorrow. Then I wouldn't have to go through it all. It would all be over and I wouldn't have had to be part of it. He closed the boots into his hands and drifted off into a deep sleep.

He woke up to sunshine streaming in through the window. His first thought was: it's here. Saturday is here. Today is my great ordeal. He sat up in bed. There was a strange stiffness in his joints. He felt a stab of pain as he moved his right knee. He was aware also of a dull, bruising ache all up his left shin. He hadn't noticed either the night before.

There was something very odd for a Saturday. What was it? There was no traffic outside. He went to the bathroom, came back and slowly dressed. Kick-off was 10.30. His watch said 8.30. He had plenty of time.

He went downstairs. His mother was not in the kitchen. He made himself some toast. There was a rattling noise at the front door and a newspaper plopped through the letter box. He ignored it and went to the door of his mother's bedroom.

'Mum, is my kit ready?' he shouted. No answer. 'Mum. My kit. Is it ready?'

This time there was an answer. A bump and a scrambling noise as if someone couldn't get out of bed and to the door quick enough. The door whipped open and Mrs Matthews stood there in her nightdress. 'What do you mean?' she stormed. 'I washed them for you last week and I washed them for you so you could have them clean for yesterday. If you think I'm going to wash them again you've got another think coming.'

'But Mum . . .' Andy started — but the door was slammed in his face.

What am I going to do? he thought. What's she talking about? I wasn't playing yesterday.

He picked up the paper. It was a *Sunday Mirror*. On the sports page was a headline UNITED GO TWO POINTS CLEAR. He winced at a twinge from his knee — which, he saw, was swollen. In the washing machine he found his football kit, caked with mud.

Disconsolately, he wandered down strangely quiet roads to school. It was deserted. The gates were locked.

He could see that the goal nets and corner posts were not in place but the grass was all churned up. But nobody had been allowed on the pitch between the practice match and the Cranbourne Road game.

Rain began to fall. He wandered home slowly.

His mother was up and dressed. 'Where have you been?' she demanded.

'For a walk,' was all Andy could say.

'Well, I hope you're satisfied with what you've done.' Andy stared at her. 'Oh, don't gawp at me like that. You know what I mean.' He didn't dare say, 'No, I don't'. 'You ruined everything,' she said. 'Made us look fools. And I won't forget it.' She stormed into her bedroom. There would be no Sunday dinner cooked that day, that was obvious. Because it was Sunday. It had to be. Andy went to the bedroom and sat down.

Could he have slept right through Saturday? Never. His kit was dirty, his knee swollen, his shin bruised. He must have been playing football. Had he been knocked on the head in the game, been concussed and forgotten everything? He'd read about such things. But wouldn't he have been taken to hospital? And have a headache? And stitches? But if not that, then what?

Nine o'clock came. He gave it all up and went to bed. Once again he closed the little boots in his hand. I wish I knew what did happen, he thought.

At some time during the night — he didn't know when or even if he dreamt it after all — he heard the doorbell ring and then voices: one his mother's sounding high and happy, the other a man's, somehow familiar.

He woke up to a dull day. His right knee and left shin were normal and quite painless. His watch said 8.30. There was a bustling noise in the little kitchen and as Andy washed and dressed he thought back to the previous day, which had been a very sad Sunday indeed. So today must be Monday. Back to school.

The *Daily Mirror* was on the kitchen table. The

headline on the sports page said UNITED'S BIG CHANCE TO GO TOP. He looked at the date. It was Saturday's. Andy sat down. His head was spinning again. Saturday and Sunday were reversed and he knew all about Sunday but nothing about Saturday. And then his heart sank. Today was the day he was to make a fool of himself in such a way that even his mother could never forget. He must be going to be very bad indeed then.

His mother put a boiled egg, coffee and toast in front of him. 'You need a good breakfast inside you,' she smiled. 'This is your big day. And you might have a surprise before it's over.'

Andy felt tears sting his eyes. He knew he gave his mother a rough time: it was hard for her without a husband. And she did realise after all how much he'd wanted to make the school team. But he was destined to let her down. And himself. And, therefore, his school, his team-mates, Mr Conway who had shown trust in him. The boiled egg and toast went down his gullet like iron filings.

His mother went to the airing cupboard and brought out his kit: the all-blue strip Costers Park wore — soft, warm, spotless and smelling sweetly of fabric conditioner. She put his gleaming boots in a plastic bag and the whole lot in his sports bag.

'There you are, Andy,' she said. 'Good luck.' And she kissed him on the cheek. Andy was amazed by this behaviour. What on earth am I going to do today to upset her? he thought. Just when she's like she used to be.

'Matthews,' said Mr Conway. 'Just slow it down a bit today, will you? *Think* what you're doing. Stop running around in circles like a crazed chicken.' Andy looked at him with despairing eyes. No fear of that, he thought, I couldn't raise a gallop.

Quite a reasonable crowd of pupils and parents had turned up for the game: at any other time Andy would have felt proud and happy. The whistle blew: the match was on. Within a few minutes Andy felt he may as well not be there. The rest of the team must have decided among themselves to ignore him. Nobody passed to him, nobody even spoke to him.

So round the pitch he meandered like a mobile spectator. He didn't even try to get the ball. Without that worry on his mind it was amazing what he saw. He knew Cranbourne Road were going to score after ten minutes and if they'd listened to him they could have marked the danger man out of the game. But they were so busy playing. So poor old Leggy Bowser in goal had no chance. Andy just kept wandering and keeping his eyes open. No huffing and puffing, no running round in circles today. He was not a bit surprised when a loose ball ran in front of him just outside the Cranbourne Park penalty area, he swung his right leg lazily at it and it was in the back of the net in a flash.

'What a fluke,' said someone. 'You jammy devil,' said someone else.

The Costers Park team seemed quite annoyed at having equalised. Andy didn't feel particularly happy about his goal. He felt so detached that he hardly noticed it. Nor was he very elated when just before half-time he did exactly the same thing again.

Mr Conway found it hard in the interval to convince his team they were doing well. 'You're in the lead,' he said. 'Two really well-taken goals.'

'Dangleboots is useless, sir. He's wandering round in a dream.'

'He's scored both goals,' said Mr Conway.

'Dead lucky. He's done nothing else, sir.'

'Jimmy Greaves used to be like that,' said Mr Conway. 'He could go through a game and only touch the ball three times and score a hat-trick.'

'That's different, sir.'

'How?' said Mr Conway. The trouble was, Andy didn't believe Mr Conway either.

'See, Matthews?' said Mr Conway. 'I told you what could happen if you slowed it down.'

It wasn't until Andy had actually scored a hat-trick with his third touch of the ball that he began to think there might be something in it. He woke up. He began to run around. He huffed and puffed. He took a kick on the shin and a knock on the knee. He began to think he wasn't going to make a fool of himself after all. He ignored Mr Conway's warning shouts from the touchline. He began to hear some other shouts from behind the goal he was attacking.

'Come on, Andy, keep hitting them. The goals will come.'

The rest of the Costers Park team had woken up to the fact that Andy might be worth playing with after all. He began to receive the ball more often and was playing as he always did. Within three minutes he had knocked over a corner flag, hit a dog and the top deck of a passing bus.

'Cool it, Andy,' yelled Mr Conway.

'Bash away at 'em, Andy,' came the voice from behind the goal. It was a voice Andy knew. He looked toward where it came from. And his heart leapt.

There stood his father. 'Get stuck in, Andy,' he bawled. 'Blast away. You could have six.'

'Dad!' yelled Andy and nearly ran off the pitch.

'Matthews,' shouted Mr Conway. 'The game isn't

over yet.'

Great, thought Andy. Dad's back. Now I've really got someone to play for. Andy was in the Cranbourne penalty area; the ball came over from the left. Andy had plenty of room. He brought the ball down, turned and hit it sweetly with his right foot. Even as the ball left his boot he knew it was travelling like a rocket. The goalkeeper dived hopelessly. But the shot was just a little off target. The ball shaved the outside of the post and, still rising, hit Andy's father full in his unprotected face.

The man fell like a stone. People gathered round: Andy fought his way through to where his father lay. Blood was pouring from his nose: there was already a livid bruise welling up under his eye. He was unconscious.

'Best get an ambulance. He could have a fracture,' said someone.

By the time the ambulance had arrived and taken Andy's father away the game was over. Costers Park held out and Mr Conway seemed reasonably pleased. No one suggested Andy should go in the ambulance with his father.

Andy tore home as quick as he could after the game. He had to tell his mum — but the house was empty and the neighbour who had the key to let him in only knew his mother had rushed off in the Mini after receiving a telephone call. The hospital was miles away; he'd never get there on his own.

Everything was rotten. He'd made a mess of it all.

At six o'clock his mother entered. She had obviously been crying.

'There you are,' she said. 'Don't talk to me.'

'Dad's back,' said Andy.

'Shut up,' she said. 'You've done enough harm for one day.'

'How do you know?' said Andy, puzzled.

'Oh, God.' Words seemed to fail her. 'He rings up late last night. Says he's coming back. That's all I've wanted for two years.'

You could have fooled me, thought Andy. Adults are past understanding.

'And he comes round this morning. He asks where you are. I tell him you're playing for the school. And I've never seen a man look so happy. "I'm off to watch him," he says. And what do you do? You try to kill him.'

'You knew he was home?' said Andy.

'Of course I did,' she said. 'You clumsy *fool*.'

'I didn't mean to do it,' said Andy in anguish. That was two people he'd laid out that week, and he hadn't meant either.

'So I go to hospital. And when he comes round he looks at me and says, "So that's my welcome? You've made him hate me. I wouldn't come back now for all the tea in China." We'll never see him again and it's *all your fault*.'

'But, Mum . . .' began Andy.

'Leave me alone — I'm going to bed.'

So that explained Sunday. It was just as well he'd not known what Saturday had brought forth. He went to bed himself and lay awake looking at the ceiling and clutching the boots. Don't let tomorrow be Sunday again, he thought. I couldn't stand it.

He woke up to another sunny morning. Even as he

opened his eyes his unhappiness hit him. Dad would never come back now. The radio was on in the kitchen — an unusual thing. He didn't have to wonder what day it was because the Radio 1 announcer clearly told him it was Monday. He slouched into the kitchen — and got the shock of his life.

'Hello, Andy. Admiring your handiwork?' His father sat at the table eating scrambled egg. One side of his face was swollen and a mixture of yellow and black.

But he's not coming back, thought Andy, amazed. Then he remembered. That was the day before yesterday. The real last thing he'd heard had been the doorbell ringing, his mother's voice sounding happy and a man's in answer. That was last night.

'You're back,' was all he could say. His mother appeared, smiling as he had never seen her.

'I was a bit muzzy Saturday,' said Dad. 'Said a few things I didn't mean. You gave me a fair welt.'

Andy hardly dared ask. 'Will you stay?'

'May as well. With a striker like you in the house.'

Andy set off for school deep in thought. The two things he'd wanted most had amazingly happened at once. 'Slow it down,' Mr Conway had said. And he had. The result? He was a real striker. Not like Johnny Caistor. But good enough. And as for the rest?

Well, there was one thing certain. He'd hang on to those dangleboots.

Pondering

Andy sat on his bed examining the dangleboots.

Was Dad back and Andy the hat-trick hero because of those nondescript little plastic objects? It couldn't be. Now Andy looked at them carefully, he was disappointed. They certainly weren't made from leather from the World Cup Final ball. Instead they were just black plastic. The tiny studs were moulded into the soles. Not a stitch to be seen. Mass-produced rubbish. So much for all that about the feet of dead great players.

And they weren't even new. Scuffed; white stripes fading — 80p down the drain. He'd been rooked.

And yet. How else could he have got two days the wrong way round? How else could what he wanted just happen? The dangleboots were the only new element in his life. They *must* be the reason.

So. If they worked once they could work again. Johnny Caistor held no more fears. Better days lay ahead. If he really wanted something, the dangleboots would get it — though he might be surprised at how. He drew in his breath with contentment — he had a secret weapon.

Andy turned away then so he didn't see the dangleboots stir and do a little silent dance on the

bed. Tiny movements from tiny boots — but if they had been full size with feet inside and kicked you, they'd have broken your ankle.

Dangleboots and the original thoughts

The man with leathery skin and the woman with dark eyes set up their stall each Saturday in a part of the market place where few people came. Their mascots, their talismen, their lucky charms were seldom sold. Whenever someone ventured across and bought something it was not replaced. The man and the woman left the space it occupied vacant.

So the nail sticking out of a roof support was bare — as it had been since the day Andy Matthews bought the little black dangleboots with the three white bands across the instep which used to hang from it.

'I wonder what he has found out,' the man would sometimes say.

'I wonder if he will come back to tell us,' the woman would answer.

Dad was home again; the Matthews family was the happier for it. But his first task had been to sign on at the DHSS. His second was to look for a job. This was hard.

'I'm a good brickie,' he said. 'But where's the building work round here?'

'Johnny Caistor's dad runs a building firm,' said Andy.

Johnny Caistor, the brilliant striker, who did every thing better than Andy. Johnny Caistor, who had named Andy 'Dangleboots' long before he had been to the market stall. Johnny Caistor, who was into everything.

'I've seen him,' said Dad. 'Nothing doing.'

'Something'll turn up,' said Mum.

'It had better,' said Dad.

Andy took the little black dangleboots out of his pocket — his mother had finally persuaded him not to hang them over the driver's mirror of the old red Mini.

'What about it, boots?' he said. 'Can you try again?'

Costers Park School. Mr Conway refereeing a practice match with his first team hopefuls.

'Nice try, Andy,' he said. 'At least you've got some power in your shooting now.'

But not much direction. The ball was lodged in the branches of the old beech tree which overlooked the changing rooms. So the game had to stop again because of Andy. First, he'd had to climb over the railings and on to the road after he had smashed the ball against the concrete lamp standard outside and seen it bounce away nearly out of sight. Now they made him climb up into the tree, which groaned ominously while he clambered clumsily.

'That old thing's rotten,' said someone. 'It ought to be chopped down.'

So did Dangleboots,' said Johnny Caistor. 'Dangleboots is a wally.'

Andy reached out and tapped at the ball. It dropped to the ground and bounced twice before Mr Conway picked it up. Then, as if to prove the previous remark,the branch Andy sat on cracked loudly. Andy

came to rest on the ground with it. He picked himself up, unhurt.

'You're right; it's dangerous,' said Mr Conway. 'I'll see the Head about it.'

'You're still a wally, Dangleboots,' said Johnny Caistor. 'You'll never change. Once a wally, always a wally.'

Dad was holding forth to Andy as they kicked a ball to each other outside the lock-up garages. Andy had told him how Johnny Caistor was always on at him.

'Don't worry, son.' *Crash* against the steel up-and-over doors. 'Don't let them get to you.' *Bang*. 'Be yourself.' *Smash*. 'Be original.' *Clang*. 'Think for yourself.' *Thud*. 'It's the only way to get on.' *Clatter*. 'Original thoughts are the only thoughts which get things done. Think them.' *Doinngg*.

'I'll try,' said Andy.

Thump. Over the garage roof. End of game.

Miss Brent was new to teaching. She found Andy's class a real handful. 'Five minutes to go,' she said. 'One-word-stories to finish off.'

Great, thought Andy.

The story started at the front of the room.

'Once.'

'There.'

'Was.'

'A.'

'Girl.'

'And.'

'She.'

'Sat.'

'By.'

'The.'

'River.'

'And.'

'She.'

'Got.'

'Pushed.'

'In.'

'And.'

'She.'

Andy's turn. Be original. Be original.

'Drowned,' he said.

The class groaned.

'Thanks, Dangleboots,' said Johnny Caistor, whose turn was next.

'Ah, well,' said Miss Brent. 'No time to start another. Let's have funny book titles instead.'

'*Dangleboots' Diary of Disaster. Volume 12*,' shouted Johnny Caistor.

The class roared with laughter.

'I don't think that's very humorous, Johnny,' said Miss Brent.

Neither did Andy.

'You know what I mean,' said Miss Brent. 'A title with a jokey name. Like *Breaking Windows* by Eva Brick.'

Mild titters sounded round the room. Johnny put his hand up. Miss Brent ignored it.

'Come on,' she said. 'Someone besides Johnny.'

Nobody moved.

'Miss, miss,' shouted Johnny. 'Here's a *great* one.'

'All right, Johnny.'

'*Mysterious Murders* by Hugh Dunnett.'

Everybody laughed.

'Very good, Johnny,' said Miss Brent. 'Now, someone else, please.'

The room hummed with the sound of brains being

racked. I'll think of one, thought Andy. Now I'll be original. All I have to do is choose a name which sounds like something else. The thing it's got to do with becomes a surname and then thinking up the title is dead easy.

Johnny's hand was in the air again.

'Miss, miss!'

'Come on, class,' said Miss Brent. 'Someone else besides Johnny.'

No reply.

'All right, Johnny.' A distinct note of reluctance in Miss Brent's voice.

'*Mini skirts for Ever* by Seymour Legg,' Johnny shouted.

Andy took time off from working out a title of his own to envy Johnny once again for being so brilliant. The whole class was rocking with laughter, and Johnny's face was split with a grin Andy would cheerfully have put his boot through.

Miss Brent didn't look too pleased at the last offering: when the laughter stopped she said, 'Surely you aren't going to leave it all to Johnny? Somebody else *must* have one.'

Andy was ready. He'd worked one out. It was great. He put up his hand.

'Well done, Andy,' said Miss Brent. 'Let's have your title.'

A big moment. Twenty pairs of eyes were on him. Twenty pairs of ears were going to hear his own completely original effort.

'Come on, Andy,' said Miss Brent.

Andy cleared his throat. He spoke.

'*How to tie things together* by Hank Ofrope.'

Silence.

'Eh?' said Johnny.

'I'm afraid I don't quite understand,' said Miss Brent, embarrassed.

'You're daft, Dangleboots,' a very audible voice said from the other side of the room.

'But it's good, Miss,' said Andy. 'Hank is a name like cowboys have.' That was true, wasn't it? In all the Westerns he'd seen everyone who wasn't called Chuck seemed to be called Hank. And what about Hank Marvin? 'And Hank is to do with rope,' he said. 'You can buy rope in hanks.' Sudden doubt. You can, can't you? Yes, he was sure you could. So 'Of rope' was a surname. No dafter than some, he was sure.

'Well, it's very ingenious, Andy,' said Miss Brent doubtfully.

'It's useless,' said a voice.

'It's cracked,' said another.

'That's enough of that,' said Miss Brent.

'It's typical Dangleboots,' said Johnny.

Miss Brent was obviously going to forget Andy's title.

'Come on, class,' she said. 'Let's have one more before break.'

Johnny put his hand up yet again.

'*Personal Computers* by Mike Rowe,' he called.

Andy put his head in his hands.

'How does he do it?' he said underneath his breath.

'You don't want to worry about him,' said Dad.

Andy was home and telling his parents about Johnny's new triumph.

'He's the best striker in the school and he keeps me out of the team and now he makes up these dead good titles on the spot while I do useless ones nobody laughs at.'

'Pretend he's not there,' said Mum.

'I can't,' said Andy. 'He's *always* there.'

'He didn't make those titles up,' said Dad. 'Everybody knows them.'

'I don't,' said Andy.

'You should read a bit more, love,' said Mum.

'Yours was far better than his,' said Dad. 'No comparison.'

'But nobody laughed at it,' said Andy.

'No matter,' said Dad. 'You made yours up. He didn't. So yours was best.'

'Tell that to the class,' muttered Andy.

'No need,' said Dad. 'Yours was original. Like I said, what's original is best. Always. Don't forget it.'

In his room Andy looked at the little dangleboots.

'Come on,' he said, 'You helped me once. Help me again. Dad wants a job. I want to be original.'

There was football practice after school. The rain was sheeting down, so Mr Conway kept the first team squad, of which Andy was now a member, indoors and talked about tactics.

Andy made himself concentrate as Mr Conway spoke.

'Most teams nowadays play 4-4-2 or sometimes, 4-3-3. It's only the Brazilians and the like who'd dare play 4-2-4. Everybody wants to defend.'

Something sounded a bit wrong with that. Andy left off his mental musings on what constituted true originality to ask a question.

'Please, sir,' he said.

'Yes, Andy?'

'4-4-2 and 4-3-3 and all those add up to ten.'

'Well done, Andy,' said Mr Conway.

'But, sir, there's eleven in a football team.'

Jeering laughter broke out.

'Prat, Dangleboots,' said someone.

'It's asking the poor devils a lot to take the field without a goalkeeper,' said Mr Conway. 'What would we do without Leggy Bowser here?'

The fat Leggy Bowser simpered. Andy thought he'd better shut up.

'When I was your age, it was all different,' said Mr Conway. 'You'd buy a programme at a football match and you wouldn't find the teams just listed on the back page. No, you'd find them on the centre pages. And they'd be all laid out like a plan of the field. Home team on top — goalie, two backs, three half-backs, five forwards. Away team underneath — five forwards, three halves, two backs, one goal keeper. And in between the two centre-forwards where the ball should be there was always an advertisement for Gillette razor blades so it looked as if the team were about to slice each other in pieces. 2–3–5. It seems prehistoric now.'

Andy sat up. A light flashed in his mind. He'd got it. AN ORIGINAL THOUGHT. It would revolutionise the game.

'Sir,' he said.

'Yes, Andy,' said Mr Conway.

'Instead of all this 4-4-2 and such, why don't teams play 0-0-10?'

'Eh?' said Mr Conway.

'It would be great,' said Andy, warming to his theme. 'It stands to reason. You'd have ten players attacking and the other team couldn't stand up to them. You'd be in their half all the time. Whenever it looked like there's a bit of danger you would turn round and belt the ball back to the goal keeper. They might score a few, but you'd score more. You'd be winning matches 12–7 instead of 3–1.'

Mr Conway was struck dumb. One or two faces looked interested in the idea. Andy sat back with the air of one who has made a real insight.

'You're just a witless herbert, Dangleboots,' said Johnny Caistor. 'It couldn't work.'

'It *would*,' said Andy. 'What's to stop it?'

'If both teams played 0–0–10, as soon as they went into each others' half they'd have their backs to each other,' said Johnny Caistor.

Yes, there was that, of course. Still . . .

'You'd win a few games before the others cottoned on,' said Andy.

'I'd hoped for a sensible discussion,' said Mr Conway. 'You'd turn the game into a cross between American football and a tank attack by the Panzer Brigade.'

So much for originality, thought Andy. The world isn't ready for me.

That night he had a *marvellous* dream. Costers Park School, playing 0–0–10, beat Arsenal 26–19. Andy scored twelve. Johnny Caistor was sent off for fouling Charlie Nicholas.

'I was talking to Caistor today,' said Dad.

Andy looked up. Surely Dad wasn't complaining to Johnny's father about what happened at school.

'Next job he has, he says he'll take me on. Now all he's got to do is to find something to build.'

Inside Andy's pocket, the dangleboots seemed to move slightly of their own accord.

Andy woke up still cross. Originality did not seem to get him very far. Two great ideas seen as mad. But they *weren't*. How to prove it?

A vague idea began to form in his mind. Remembering something, he looked in the cupboard where Mum kept a lot of bits and pieces for the house. Yes, he was right. Thin, very strong nylon rope; coiled neatly round itself and bound with a paper sleeve with SUPERIOR CLOTHES LINE printed on it. Great. A Hank of Rope. A sticker on the sleeve saying 'Special Offer. Half Price' made him look deeper in the cupboard. Yes. He knew his mother. She'd bought two while she was about it.

So. Andy rehearsed the scene in his mind, before a wondering, contrite crew headed by Johnny Caistor. 'These are *banks* of *rope*. And I can use them for *tying* things *together*. So my title might not be very funny but it does make sense so it was a lot cleverer than the drivel you came out with.'

Andy felt much better after that. So he stuck both clothes lines in his bag, made sure the dangleboots were in his pocket and started out for school.

All his life, Len Symes had wanted to be a bus driver. And now, at last, his ambition was coming true. On this sunny morning he reached the bus garage. His step was light. Today was a good day. For the first time he would take a double-decker bus out on the open road. L-plates and a *Driver under instruction* sign would mean that no member of the public need risk life by sharing the experience.

The old bus, a low-geared chugger with its separate driver's cab — it was one of the very few two-man vehicles left in the company waited for him.

Andy bided his time. The morning passed uneventfully. All shafts of humour directed at him were ignored. The clothes line stayed in his bag.

Len Symes did a morning run round the town. Nothing happened to disturb his concentration or worry the men on the lower deck watching every move he made.

'Good lad, Len,' said one when they were back at the depot. 'This afternoon we'll take her out again.'

Andy knew they would be at him in the dinner hour. Johnny Caistor had worked out this new chant. He took Mr Conway's remark about American football and the Panzer Brigade and fixed it to the first name in Andy's title. He had come up with something everybody would want to shout.

'Hank, Hank, the Yanky Tank.'

It went on and on.

They were all out by the changing rooms. Ten yards away was the fence by the main road. On the other side of the changing rooms was the old beech tree.

Andy had his bag with him. He faced his tormentors. In his pocket the dangleboots once again seemed to move slightly. He pulled out the two coils of clothes line.

'All right,' he yelled. The noise quietened. Everybody looked at him. The thought that there might be some more entertainment crossed a lot of minds.

'See these?' he shouted, holding up the clothes

lines. 'What are they?'

He went on quickly before anyone could give him an answer.

'They're *banks*. They're *banks* of *rope*. Now who's being stupid?'

The laughter that answered was of disbelief. Andy felt he wasn't quite making his point.

'And this is what you do with them,' he continued tearing off the paper sleeves and uncoiling the rope. He rushed over to the fence, half climbed it so he could lean over and looped one end of the rope round the concrete lamp-post. He tied a reef-knot, pulled it to make sure it wouldn't slip, dashed back and did the same with the other end to the open window frame in the changing-room wall.

Then he looked again at the crowd watching him. They returned his gaze, struck dumb by this amazing behaviour.

'See?' said Andy.

Obviously they didn't. So he took the other clothes line, tied that also round the window frame, rushed over to the beech tree, looped the rope round its trunk, tied another reef-knot and, empty handed, came back to where he was before.

'Look,' he said, pointing backwards and speaking very slowly as if to idiots. '*Tying things together by Hank Ofrope*. You didn't have to laugh.'

Nobody did. Suddenly everybody seemed sympathetic. Johnny Caistor came up to Andy, put an arm round his shoulders and said. 'We're not laughing, Dangleboots. And after school we'll play football and your side can play 0–0–10.'

Something told Andy he shouldn't enquire too much about this sudden change of heart.

Len Symes's bus took the right hand turn on to the ring road which in half an hour would bring him past Costers Park School.

Mr Conway was surprisingly easy to persuade. 'Keep 'em happy,' was his watchword.

So there they were: two teams, one pledged to play ordinarily, the other with a goal keeper and ten forwards, Andy leading from the middle.

'No one's taken your ropes down,' said Johnny Caistor as he and Andy faced each other at the kick off.

Andy looked at his square confident face. Perhaps having a Gillette razor blade instead of a ball might in some circumstances be preferable.

Len Symes whistled as his bus rattled along. He'd got the hang of his machine all right.

Andy kicked off. His ten man forward line surged forward. The ball was lost at once; it came to Johnny Caistor who raced through on his own and scored.

'All thanks to Dangleboots, the tactical genius,' he shouted.

From the kick-off he got the ball at once and did the same thing once more.

But it *must* work, thought Andy. Johnny Caistor just doesn't see the point of it.

Within two minutes Johnny Caistor had done it again.

'Keep hold of the ball,' shouted Andy, to his team. 'We *must* score. Sheer weight of numbers.

The bus turned the corner and started to pass in front of the school building.

This time there would be no mistake. Andy's forwards swept down field like a tidal wave, a moving brick wall. Somewhere along the line was the ball. No one knew where. Andy, in the penalty area, stopped his headlong rush and looked round for it. Yes, it was bobbling around in front of him as if unsure what was supposed to happen to it in this outlandish new way of playing the game.

Andy dashed forward and swung his right leg.

Len Symes had had a really good day. He had driven perfectly and was on the way home. Suddenly he realised how hot it was in the cab. He slid the side window open and let cool air play over the side of his face.

Andy's boot made contact with the ball which flew in a dead straight line at amazing speed like a heat-seeking missile. Leggy Bowser jumped out of its way.

Len Symes whistled a happy tune.

Andy's face fell as the ball missed the goalpost, then lightened as he remembered no one was there this time to catch it in the face.

The ball carried on, over the grass, over the fence, over the road.

Len Symes was still whistling as his bus passed Costers Park School. He was proud of the way he whistled, of the fruity tone he produced, of his three-octave range, of the virtuoso leaps, runs and trills he could produce at will. He often thought he ought to enter a talent competition as the new Percy Edwards. Then he would leave the buses for good.

He essayed a really difficult trill at the highest note he could manage. He drew in his breath at the precise moment the football shot neatly through the open window and hit him on the ear.

The whistle in mid-curlicue turned to a wild shout. His hands left the steering wheel. The bus careered off the road straight into the concrete lamp-post to which Andy had tied the clothes line.

Everybody on the field turned to watch.

The lamp standard keeled over. The knot held: the clothes line tautened but did not break. Instead, there was a rumbling noise as the entire window frame it was tied to was pulled out from the wall. Bricks and cement-dust followed it and left a gaping hole at the end of the changing room.

'Oh, heck,' said Andy.

The lamp-post continued its long topple. The other clothes line went taut. A strange creaking sounded.

'It's the tree,' said Johnny Caistor.

Yes. It was even more rotten than anyone had thought. They watched the unfolding sight – the subsiding lamp-post, the straight clothes line, the window frame hanging helpless in mid-air like a strange steel kite, the beech tree slowly moving, beginning an improbably parallel topple which no one could stop as the rotten, strengthless wood underneath became visible.

Strengthless, yes – but still heavy.

'My God, the changing rooms,' yelled Mr Conway.

The dead tree teetered as the lamp standard hit the ground. Then down it came, pulled by the taut ropes straight on top of the changing room roof. The end wall, weakened by the loss of the window, collapsed. The roof followed it. Before their eyes, the changing room disappeared in a cloud of white dust which rose in a mushroom shape like a tiny atom bomb.

'Stone me,' said Len Symes, who had all the old Tony Hancock programmes on video.

'Well done, Dangleboots. It's all down to you,' said Johnny Caistor.

'I'm going home,' said Andy.

'What shall I tell the Head?' groaned Mr Conway.

Actually nothing much happened afterwards. Except that Johnny Caistor's father put in a tender to rebuild the changing room.

'He's taking me on,' said Dad. 'I'm in work again.'

The dangleboots in Andy's pocket stirred slightly as if trying to remind him of something. Andy thought for a moment. The day's memories weren't really too good. Still, credit where credit was due.

'Thanks again, boots,' he said. Then, to his father, 'You were right, Dad. It's all down to original thoughts.'

Back on the market stall the dark-eyed woman spoke to the leathery-skinned man.

'I feel it in my bones,' she said. 'He will soon be back to tell us.'

Questioning

Andy was in his room again looking at the dangleboots. Today's happenings hadn't been so good. He'd wanted to be original — and he had. Looking back on it, he thought he'd behaved like a raving lunatic. He cringed with embarrassment at the memory of dashing from tree to window to lamppost tying up the clothes line. No wonder Johnny Caistor was sympathetic. They'd only played 0–0–10 to be kind to him. And then the dangleboots had got his dad a job. Great. But was wrecking the school the ideal way to do it?

And a lot of things the dangleboots didn't seem to understand. Andy had hoped the scourge of Johnny Caistor would be wiped out. Instead, Johnny really had something on him now. Andy would have to work out very carefully what he wanted the dangleboots to do in future. If only Johnny Caistor could be made to look stupid, preferably in public; and if Andy could at the same time be in charge of things, confident, competent — the sort of person he knew inside that he really was but never got a chance to show.

Be patient, Andy said to himself. Wait for the place,

wait for the time. Then the dangleboots will show what they can do.

Dangleboots and the amazing stage effects

The note from school had only stayed in Andy's pocket for ten days before he gave it to his mother. That was pretty good for him.

The letter was about a theatre trip — cost £3 for coach and seat. Andy's father was scornful.

'What's he want to go watching a load of painted pansies ponceing around for? If the school wants him to see plays, let him watch the telly.'

'It's not the same,' said his mother.

'It's a sight better,' said his father. 'It's all recorded so you know they won't mess it up. Anyway, we can't afford it!'

Secretly, Andy really wanted to go. But he carefully made them think he wasn't bothered. He knew the signs by now. If his father was against his going, his mother would quietly slip him an envelope next morning with £3 and the signed reply slip in it. By that time his father would have gone to work; Andy would see him during the day with his brickie's trowel as the walls of the rebuilt changing rooms grew higher.

The dangleboots were securely zipped up in the pocket of Andy's bomber jacket as he walked to school. The morning was cold and dark. December was nearly here.

'Dangleboots.'

Johnny Caistor, shouting twenty metres behind him. Karen Turpin, reputed to fancy him, was by his side. Andy looked back but didn't walk slower. The others would have to catch him.

In spite of the Cranbourne Road game and although the changing room walls were only three feet high and the window frames hadn't even arrived on site yet, Johnny Caistor could not bring himself to think of Andy as anything but a prat. He hadn't forgiven him for spraining his ankle in the first place. Which is why Andy didn't slow down. But they soon caught up with him.

'You going to the play?' demanded Johnny.

Andy grunted.

'Can't hear you.'

'I said yes.'

'Good things, plays,' said Johnny. 'I don't know which I'll be. A big star on the stage and TV or a footballer and play for England.'

'Both,' said Karen Turpin.

'Perhaps I will,' said Johnny.

Andy could see Johnny Caistor was perfectly serious.

'You big head,' he said.

'Got something to be bigheaded about, haven't I?' said Johnny. 'That's more than you have.'

Karen giggled.

'I bet I could go up on that stage today,' said Johnny, 'and make all those actors there look idiots. They're nothing, they aren't. Nothing special, anyway. If they were, they'd be out of that scrap heap and away in London. No, I could show them a thing or two now, even if I am only eleven, because I've got talent.'

Actually, he was probably right. He had been Herod in the Nativity Play three years running and had scared the wits out of the infants each time.

'It's easy saying that,' said Andy. 'You won't get the chance. We're only going to watch.'

'Pity, that,' said Johnny. 'You could have come with me. That way I'd look even better.

Andy was so used to this sort of thing that he usually didn't bother to react. He was surprised at a sudden anger and wish for revenge which filled him.

The trip was that afternoon. Most of Andy's class were going. Dilip, who sat next to Andy, had also brought his money at the last possible moment.

That morning, Miss Brent told them what they were in for.

'We're going to see a new play written specially for children,' she said.

Johnny groaned exaggeratedly and muttered, 'I'd rather watch my video nasties.' Miss Brent pretended not to hear.

'It's called *The Wacky Wizard of Happy Valley* by Gus Rentgarden. It's been specially written for the theatre and you'll be seeing the first performance. So you're quite privileged.'

If Miss Brent thought that would impress her class, she was doomed to disappointment. So she went on.

'This play might be different from what you expect,' she said. 'The theatre's got a different sort of stage. So the play's being done in the round.'

There was a muffled explosion of laughter from Johnny Caistor and a gasp of what sounded like 'in the nude'. Miss Brent looked at him sternly.

'Johnny,' she said. 'I'm getting very tired of you. Any more and I won't let you come.'

'Oh, miss,' said Johnny pleadingly and winked at Karen.

'Who knows what acting a play in the round means?' said Miss Brent and looked hopefully round the room. Not a sound.

'Guess,' she said.

Still no answer.

'Andy?' said Miss Brent.

'Dangleboots knows everything,' whispered Johnny. This time, Miss Brent let it pass. She was getting quite good at knowing what to hear and what not to. She looked at Andy and seemed to expect an answer.

Andy racked his brains. It couldn't be too hard if Miss Brent thought he could guess. He thought. Theatre in the round. A peculiar vision came into his mind. Japanese Sumo wrestlers meet the Roly-Polies. Yes, that must be it.

'The actors are all so fat they're too heavy to go on an ordinary stage,' he said.

He knew Johnny Caistor would be jeering even before he had finished the sentence. The rest of the class picked up the cue and laughed. Miss Brent smiled at Andy in a way he didn't quite like — as if to say: 'Why do I keep asking you questions? Won't I ever learn?' — and said, 'Well, at least you tried, Andy.'

'He's always trying, miss,' said Karen and Johnny Caistor pushed his fist in his mouth to stop himself laughing. Miss Brent sighed. The moment she spoke to Andy, she knew someone would trot that old one out. But it was true. He was.

'Acting in the round means the audience sits in a circle round the stage. So we don't see the play like a picture or a TV screen. More like watching tennis at Wimbledon. You can look at it from any angle.'

'Sounds daft,' said Johnny Caistor.

'It's not. You'll like it,' said Miss Brent, but without much conviction.

The coach was to leave after lunch. The drive into the city would take about forty minutes. As they milled round the dining hall queuing for food, Andy saw the Head standing with a strange man — middle-aged, with glasses, thinning hair and wearing a brown suit.

Karen Turpin and Johnny were just in front of Andy in the queue. As they walked with their loaded trays to an empty table and Andy and Dilip started to follow them, Andy heard the Head speak to the strange man.

'You don't mind sitting with the kids, do you?'

A split-second look of stark horror crossed the stranger's face before he answered, 'No, not at all.'

'Karen.' The Head called and Karen turned.

'This is Mr Wheyfoot. He's an Adviser from the Education Authority, come to see what we do here. He'll be coming with you on the trip today. Take him to your table and keep him entertained, will you?'

Karen's face showed a look of horror even starker than that shown by Mr Wheyfoot. The Head saw it.

'Don't worry,' he said. 'Just tell him a few of your best rude jokes. They'll keep him happy.'

Mr. Wheyfoot was led to the end of the table. Karen sat at his right, Johnny next to her. Andy was opposite Karen and Dilip next to him. There was an awkward silence. Karen looked wildly from face to face. No help from anyone. Did the Head mean what he said? She cleared her throat.

'What's green and smells?' she said.

Johnny roared with laughter.

Andy was scandalised.

'You can't ask him that,' he said.

'Why not?' said Johnny.

'You know why not,' said Dilip.

'The Head told me to tell him some rude jokes,' said Karen.

'You can't tell him that one,' said Andy.

Karen thought. Then she started again.

'There was this honeymoon couple,' she said. 'And when they...'

Mr Wheyfoot broke in.

'I really think this conversation's gone far enough,' he said. 'I must say I'm surprised at you all.' Looking at Karen, he added, 'Especially you.'

Andy felt suddenly angry at this.

'That's not fair,' he said. 'Karen was only doing what the Head told her.'

'You couldn't have thought he was serious, surely?' said Mr Wheyfoot.

'How are we supposed to know?' said Andy. He hadn't felt so cross for a long time as he did with this peculiar person from nowhere who had been plonked down at his table. 'If a teacher tells you to do something, you've got to do it.'

'You've got a lot to learn about life,' said Mr Wheyfoot.

'You're not much help,' said Andy.

Yes, he was really surprised at just how angry he felt. That was the second time today. Anger and a wish for revenge on those who caused it.

Mr Wheyfoot raised his eyes to the ceiling.

'My God,' he said. 'Don't they teach appropriateness and register at this school?'

Nobody said a word for the rest of the lunch. They fixed their eyes on their plates and their minds on the problems posed by each separate forkful of food. It seemed like four hours before Mr Wheyfoot — with a last, long, backward look at Andy — was whisked away by the Head for a cup of coffee.

Johnny laughed.

'I bet you're for it now,' he said to Andy.

'At least he spoke up for me,' said Karen. 'Him and Dilip. That's more than you did.'

I bet *he* doesn't always say the right thing, thought Andy. I'd love to see the pompous twit make a real fool of himself.

The coach waited at the front of the school. Miss Brent and Mr Conway were in charge of the party. As the kids filed in, the driver turned round to watch them.

'Hullo, Len,' said Johnny Caistor.

For it was indeed Len Symes, who had passed his test and got his PSV licence in spite of writing off a double-decker bus. He hadn't realised where he was bringing his coach until he turned into the school entrance. It was too late to turn back. He scanned the children as they entered. When he saw Andy, he turned pale and said, 'You sit at the back, as far from me as you can. You're a bleeding walking accident, you are.'

Once more, Andy was surprised at feeling the same niggle of anger and wish to get his own back as he had felt that day already over Johnny and Mr Wheyfoot. As if something was building up inside him. He made sure the dangleboots were safely in his pocket. Then he shrugged his shoulders and went obligingly to the back seat, next to Dilip, where they could spend the journey seeing where they had been. They were too far away to hear Len's ceaseless whistling.

As the road unwound behind them, he thought. Wait for the place; wait for the time. Pity it couldn't be this afternoon. They'd have an audience all right.

They left the coach in a lorry park close by the theatre. The last they saw of Len Symes was, whistling silenced, leaning back in a passenger seat, hands behind his back, preparing for a quick kip. A thermos of tea was placed on one side of him; on the other was the *Sun* open at the racing page ready for the radio commentaries he would switch on later. He'd been to the betting shop before he picked the coach up from the depot. His afternoon would be a good one — he hoped.

Miss Brent and Mr Conway shepherded their flock along the streets to the theatre. Inside, it was as Miss Brent had suggested. Steeply-raked seats surrounded a stage on which there was a staircase. At the top was what looked like a garden shed with no walls. The theatre was still nearly empty and very cold. The Costers Park party sat in its seats facing the garden shed and shivered.

Other school parties came in. There was whispered, embarrassed conversation all round. It died of its own accord and hundreds of eyes looked at the empty open stage. Two stage hands entered with large brooms and carefully swept it. They left. Eyes kept staring in stony silence.

The puzzled voice of an infant sitting next to Miss Brent sounded out very clearly.

'Miss, has it started yet?'

Before Miss Brent could say, 'Not yet, Emma,' everything suddenly went pitch black. At the same time a great noise — a drum roll, cymbals clashing, many voices shouting a wordless chant which moved upwards and upwards to be cut off all at once and be succeeded by silence. And the lights went up with a shocking brilliance which made everybody blink.

And what a sight. Twenty actors wearing shining robes of green, red, yellow and purple stood round the stage facing inwards. Their arms were raised imploringly towards what no longer looked like a garden shed but a pagoda, its pitched roof twinkling with myriad lights. And into this pagoda slowly strode a huge, bearded figure in a white robe shot with luminous red stars and a tall pointed hat. Presumably the Wacky Wizard himself.

'Brilliant,' Andy breathed.

So the play unfolded. It appeared that the Wacky Wizard and his apprentices (the ones in robes all round the stage) were imprisoned in their College of Sorcery in Happy Valley by a race of evil, goblin-like creatures called Narcs under their leader Grandnarc the Crass. Such was the power of evil possessed by the Narcs that all the Wizard's spells were rendered useless unless he could rediscover the Secret Stone of Happy Valley hidden by a Wacky Wizard of long ago. The powers of this stone were only to be called upon when Happy Valley was in its hour of greatest need. However, the present Wacky Wizard's grandfather (Wackiest of all the Wizards) had unfortunately lost the instructions about how to find it. Its rediscovery and the vanquishing of the Narcs was to be the story of the play.

'This is crap,' said Johnny Caistor.

'Sssh!' said Mr Wheyfoot, whose face wore a look of delighted anticipation.

The Narcs, when they appeared, did indeed look pretty evil. They wore black leotards and what looked like plastic bin-liners. They also looked suspiciously like the Wizard's apprentices. When apprentices and Narcs fought, both teams seemed to be at half strength. Grandnarc the Crass looked like nothing on earth in voluminous black robes and a black crash helmet with a great beak stuck on the front which made speech difficult. The voice, when it was heard, also defied expectation because it was a woman's. This delighted Karen but audibly disgusted Johnny Caistor.

Mr Conway turned round.

'You keep your comments to yourself, Caistor, or you'll be off for an early bath,' he said.

Andy, meanwhile, thought it was all great. The swirling colours of the apprentices and the black of the massed Narcs, the fights, the songs, the dances, the great shouted speeches, above all the mighty contest between the Wacky Wizard and Grandnarc the Crass — all held him rapt. He had to shake his head to bring himself back into the real world when the lights went up, the interval came and Happy Valley was again an empty stage with a garden shed on it — though now, it seemed, a doomed garden shed.

Miss Brent, down at the front with the infants, looked round.

'Well, what do you think?' she said.

'It's fantastic,' said Andy.

'It's useless,' said Johnny.

'There is an exciting raw power in the verse,' said Mr Wheyfoot. 'Personally, I find the whole concept, viewed as an extended metaphor of the struggle between good and evil, successful at many levels.'

Mr Conway gave him a peculiar look and said to Johnny, 'Make sure you keep your trap shut in the second half.'

When the stage lights came up again after the interval, the scene was deserted. Solemn notes from the synthesiser showed the depth of despair the Wizard's supporters had reached. The Wizard himself appeared under the roof of his pagoda and, slowly, draggingly, descended the staircase to speak directly to the audience.

Our world of summer's gone: the winter frost
Mocks all we were and shows us what we've lost.
No magic spell can rid us of our woe;
No runes from me can cause this curse to go.
No help will come: alone we must all wait
Until the Narcs will deal to us our fate.

Here he paused and walked to and fro across the stage, head in hands. Then he straightened and spoke to each part of the audience in turn. To those on his right, he said:

But what is this I'm saying? I the Wizard
Doubting my own powers to conquer? This is a d-
Readful weakness I'm confessing. I should be
Shot, and if my helpers heard me, probably would
be.

He walked across to his left and declaimed to those on that side.

If only we could find the Secret Stone.
The secret's lost, though. Not by thought alone
Will we discover it. Magic too must serve.
But though I try with every sinew, nerve
And strength I have, my magic's gone for ever.
No magic, then no stone; no stone, then never
Will we rid ourselves of Narcs. We're doomed.
Unless there is some other way I cannot even
Guess.

Now he crossed to the edge of the stage in front of his Pagoda, so he was facing the Costers Park party head on.

There's other magic in the world — I know it.
The time's ripe for the rest of the world to show it.
New blood must be brought in to Happy Valley
New Wizards trained, new spells worked out. Who'll rally
To our cause and join us? Who will rise,
Come to me here and look me in the eyes?

The Costers Park crew looked alarmed. The Wizard wanted some of them to go on stage. Everybody tried to avoid his eyes; fingernails were examined, stage lights counted.

'I wish I were your age again,' said Mr Wheyfoot. 'I'd be up there like a shot.'

Andy alone stayed looking straight ahead. The dangleboots still in his bomber jacket pocket seemed to move of their own accord again. The Wizard's eyes met his. Slowly Andy rose and walked with measured tread down the gangway.

Why am I doing this? I must be mad, he thought. But a voice inside him seemed to say, *It is your destiny*. The stage came nearer. The Wizard pranced joyfully round it shouting his head off.

Praise be. The first who'll save our state is here.
He's coming. Now then, friends, give him a cheer.

The cheers which swept round the theatre were of relief. One of the Wizard's apprentices came down the steps with a bundle. When Andy reached the Wizard, the bundle was unwrapped. It contained a white cloak with red stars and a pointed hat — just like the Wizard's. The apprentice helped Andy on with them. They were hot and heavy and he felt strange. The dangleboots in his pocket were moving quite frenziedly, like water-divining rods.

The Wizard turned back to the audience.

I need another. One is not enough.
The tasks I'm giving them are pretty tough.

There was a disturbance in the audience and someone stood up. It was Johnny Caistor.

'I'm not letting Dangleboots get away with that,' he shouted and raced down to the stage.

Another bundle was produced; Johnny put the robes and hat on and the two small wizards looked at each other.

'I knew we'd get on stage together,' said Johnny. 'Now watch me go.'

Andy didn't answer. But he knew. The place and time were here. Under his robes he unzipped his bomber jacket pocket, took out the dangleboots and closed them in his hand. Something good was going to happen.

On the stage it was very hot. Up close, the Wizard's face sweated through his make-up and the staircase was made of nothing more than stage blocks just like those back at school. But it was still an unnerving place with bright lights beating down and hundreds of watching faces stretching back into blackness.

The Wizard, for the moment, had no more speeches. First, he got the boys to tell everybody their names and schools. The idea must have been to stop them being nervous. It didn't altogether work. While Johnny shouted his out in a clear, confident voice, Andy mumbled.

The Wizard whispered to both of them.

'Don't worry. Just do what I tell you and don't try any funny stuff. Can you both read?'

Andy nodded because it seemed a sensible question. Johnny said, ''Course I can flaming well read. Who do you think I am?'

'All right, you can start, then,' said the Wizard. He gave Johnny a black wand with a silver star on one end. On the star was stuck a square of paper with writing on it. 'Look this over and read it when I tell you.'

He gave Andy a similar wand with no writing. Then he turned again to the audience and started declaiming once more.

Now Happy Valley's champions start their task.
Their powers are fresh and strong. All that I ask
They'll do. One of them here to read the spell,
(here he pointed to Johnny)
The other, there, to do it. Wish them well.

He turned to Johnny.

'Now,' he shouted.

While Johnny read the words on the wand, the Wizard muttered to Andy.

'All you've got to do is to wave the wand and shout two words. They're the last two words he's going to say. I'll say them when he's finished, then you say them and wave the wand. The words are, "he did". Get it?'

'I think so,' said Andy.

Meanwhile, Johnny was reading his words, and making a real meal of them — belting them out at the top of his voice.

Mr Conway passed his hand wearily over his forehead.

'He thinks he's Herod again,' he murmured.

Our Stone was lost long years ago.
Who by? A Wacky Wizard of past ages,
The wackiest of all these sages.
But still the only man to know
Its secrets. He's the only one
Who'll help us get our great work done.
So bring him here,
Let him appear
To answer for what he did.

By the time the Wizard had finished giving his instructions, Andy was only able to take in the last three lines. Yes, he thought. There's a few people I'd like to make appear to answer for what they did. Did to me. Those who've upset me today for a start. Len Symes. And that Adviser bloke.

'He did,' roared the Wizard.

Yes, that would be great. That strange, mutinous feeling Andy had had three times already that day returned stronger than ever. The dangleboots

danced.

Andy felt a dig in the ribs and a whispered 'Come on.'

'He did,' he managed to shout and waved the wand wildly.

What should have happened now was a loud explosion and a puff of smoke from behind the Pagoda. When it cleared, there, walking down the steps, would be an ancient version of the Wacky Wizard brought back from the past.

There was a bang all right. But it came from right between them. And when the smoke cleared, there on stage was Len Symes — sitting on his coach seat, thermos in one hand, mug in the other, in mid-pour, with from somewhere over his head a voice shouting, 'And they're under starter's orders. And they're off. And coming up to the first flight of fences, in the lead is . . .'

Len stared wildly round. His eyes took in three frightening figures in robes and pointed hats. One of them he knew. He screamed.

'Help. Keep him away from me. He's dangerous.'

He tried to scramble out of his seat. He couldn't. He was stuck fast.

'What am I doing here?' he shouted.

No one could answer. But the dangleboots seemed to be trying to kick their way out of Andy's hands. Poor old Len, thought Andy. He didn't upset me that much. Not as much as that Mr Wheyfoot. The dangleboots stopped moving. Almost as if they were listening to his thoughts. Len sat back and seemed to drift into some sort of coma. The lights round him dimmed. For the moment he was a forgotten shadow.

The theatre was in uproar. Kids were standing on

their seats cheering. Mr Wheyfoot nudged Mr Conway and said, 'Seldom have I seen such remarkable stage effects as in this production. I really must find time to congratulate the Company personally.'

Under cover of the noise, the Wizard got Andy and Johnny together. He was shaking.

'God knows what all that was about,' he said. 'And I don't think I want to. We'll start again.'

When it was quiet enough, Johnny went through his speech once more. This time, the end went much better. Johnny shouted:

So bring him here,
Make him appear
To answer for what he did.

'He did,' bellowed the Wizard.

'He did,' yelped Andy, heaving the wand around.

Another loud report. And when the smoke cleared, there sat Mr Wheyfoot on the stage. In the auditorium, Mr Conway looked down at the smoke coming out of the screwholes where his seat had been fastened.

Mr Wheyfoot blinked. Amazing. One second he was sitting next to Mr Conway planning how to go back-stage afterwards without holding the Costers Park party up too much; the next he was sitting in the middle of that very same stage. 'I'd be up there like a shot,' he had said. And here he was. How marvellously fortunate.

Well, no moment like the present. The Wizard towered over him. Mr Wheyfoot didn't think of him as the Wacky Wizard but as Redvers Rundle, who had done big parts in Shakespeare and one-man shows at the Edinburgh Festival. This was too good a chance to miss.

'Mr Rundle,' he said. 'Do you see a continuity between work in children's theatre such as this and the mainstream classical repertoire?'

The Wizard looked round helplessly.

'Get him off,' he shouted.

'It occurs to me,' said Mr Wheyfoot, 'that the direct actor-child contact in this sort of production — exemplified by the present encounter, I may say — bears a close relationship to the rapport with the audience you build up so effectively in your one-man shows and, it need hardly be said, in the major Shakespearian soliloquies.'

The Wizard strode in front of Mr Wheyfoot and hid him with his robes. A muffled voice carried on.

'On the other hand, it may be that the broad, unsubtle acting techniques you are employing in this particular role are different in kind from your work with, say, the National Theatre or the RSC.'

Oh, heck, thought Andy. The dangleboots have done it again. They're making Len and Mr Wheyfoot pay all right for what they said to me. And how neatly! Mr Wheyfoot had criticised the kids for using the wrong sort of talk at the wrong time. And what was he doing now? Making himself look a real prat doing just the same. And when he got back to his seat, he'd KNOW!

But not yet. Mr Wheyfoot freed himself from the Wizard's robes and looked out. And what did he see? Faces in rows stretching away into darkness. An audience.

'Just what I've always wanted,' he said and stood up.

Len Symes realised the same thing at the same moment. A big audience, a packed audience, an audience who wouldn't go away. At last. *My whistling career starts here*, he thought. Now he found he could move. So he also stood up. And now Len Symes and Mr Wheyfoot stood together.

Len started. The Wizard was too horrified to stop him.

'Ladies and gentlemen,' he said. He'd spent hours working out this routine in the cab of his bus. 'Come with me on a walk through the countryside. Listen. High up in the sky we hear the song of the nightingale.'

The infants, who by now believed everything they saw, listened. Len put his hands to his mouth and blew into them. Shrill squeaks and chirrups emerged which most were prepared to accept were like the noise made by the bird in question. Meanwhile, Mr Wheyfoot simpered and said, 'While I cannot pretend to the great talent of our famous colleague here — (Len looked pleased but Mr Wheyfoot meant the Wizard) — 'nevertheless I would like to render for you something from *Hamlet*— a person who has, I often feel, quite a lot in common with me, if I may say so.'

As Len's nightingale flew off and gave way to the barn owl searching for prey, Mr Wheyfoot faced the Costers Park party and bellowed:

Oh what a rogue and peasant slave am I . . .

'You said it,' muttered Mr Conway.

'And now we return indoors to the farmhouse,' Len declaimed, 'to find that the farmer's wife has put a record on the gramophone. Hark. What is it? Why, it is one for the old-timers. The singing strings of Mantovani echo round the kitchen.'

Now he really excelled himself with piercing notes in a descending scale which made the infants at the front stop their ears. Mr Wheyfoot suddenly realised he was not alone.

'Stop this trash,' he demanded.

'You belt up, you big fairy,' said Len. 'I was here first.'

Mr Wheyfoot took a feeble swipe at Len and missed. Len drew back his fist as if to knock Mr Wheyfoot back into his empty space in the audience.

At last the Wizard was able to stir.

'Get off,' he yelled.

Len's and Mr Wheyfoot's eyes widened, as if they both came to at the same time. They looked at each other and even under the lights everybody could see their faces flood deep red with embarrassment. The kids all round the theatre crowed with delight. It was not every day that two adults made absolute berks of themselves in such an obvious place. The two men allowed themselves to be led back to where they had come from. Len reached his marooned driver's seat to hear in the air above him the radio voice tell him his fancied horse had come last. Mr Wheyfoot lowered himself into his own seat as if it was the electric chair. And when they had sat down the dangleboots ceased their sport. A *whoosh* and a *clunk* and they were gone.

Mr Wheyfoot's seat perfectly re-entered the screw-holes in the floor. Mr Wheyfoot sat looking down, chin on chest, wishing he wasn't there. Len opened his eyes back in the coach and thought he'd had a bad dream.

The Wizard stuck to his task. 'For God's sake let's get this play moving again,' he muttered.

But it was going to take some time to calm the audience down. Meanwhile, Andy considered. The dangleboots seemed to have got out of control. How was he going to bring them back? Wait for the time, wait for the place — and here they both were. The dangleboots had just been warming up. They hadn't started on Johnny Caistor yet.

Order came back.

'Right. Pretend nothing happened. Start again,' said the Wizard to Johnny. 'Read your speech.'

'What speech?' said Johnny.

'The speech I gave you. The speech you've read twice already.'

'No, I haven't,' said Johnny.

The Wizard clapped his hand to his forehead and raised his eyes heavenwards.

'What are you trying to do to me?' he said.

'What are you talking about?' said Johnny.

The Wizard snatched the wand. He pointed to the words on the star. Johnny looked at them.

'I'm not reading that,' he said. 'It's rubbish.'

'*Read it*,' roared the Wizard.

'And so's this play. I only came up here because Dangleboots did.' Johnny was now talking very quickly, with a curious round-eyed expression on his face. 'You see, I laugh at Dangleboots a lot but inside I'm a bit afraid of him. He's not as daft as he looks. And after his three goals against Cranbourne Road I keep thinking Mr Conway might have me out of the team for good and him in. I've got to be best at everything. And everyone's got to see it. That's why I can't let him get away with anything.'

'READ THE SPEECH,' roared the Wizard.

Johnny looked at it again. A look of baffled fear crossed his face.

'I can't,' he said.

'READ THE . . .' the Wizard started.

Johnny's voice sounded terrified.

'I can't. I can't read. It's all squiggles. What's happened? I could read a few minutes ago.'

The Wizard snatched the wand from Johnny and shoved it into Andy's hands.

'You read it,' he said.

Andy did. His voice, clear and bell-like in a way which amazed him, rolled round the theatre.

Our stone was lost long years ago.
Who by? A Wacky Wizard of past ages,
The Wackiest of all these sages,
But still the only man to know
Its secrets. He's the only one
Who'll help us get our great task done.
So bring him here,
Make him appear
To answer for what he did.

'He did,' bellowed the Wizard.

There was an inaudible mutter from Johnny.

'Well done, Andy,' murmured Mr Conway. 'He's a lad of surprises.'

At last the play continued as it should. Through a billow of smoke the ancient Wizard appeared, to give up his secrets. Finally, Andy and Johnny took their robes off and went back to their seats. And as they walked together, Andy noticed something.

Johnny Caistor was crying.

'You were amazing,' said Dilip when they were back on the coach.

'Thanks,' said Andy. 'I felt really good at the end.'

Karen Turpin, in the seat in front, turned round.

'You were great,' she said. 'Much better than Johnny.'

If she's going to start fancying me, thought Andy, I'd better emigrate.

Johnny was also in the seat in front. Andy leaned over, to see him hunched up strangely and looking fixedly out of the window.

'What's up?' said Andy.

'Shut up,' said Johnny. 'Don't talk to me.'

'But I want to know what's the matter.'

Johnny turned round. Andy was shocked at the scared look in his eyes. He spoke with difficulty, as if he didn't want to say the words which haltingly came out.

'How would you like it if you suddenly found you'd forgotten how to read?'

So that was it. With Johnny, the dangleboots hadn't done anything spectacular, as they had with Len Symes and Mr Wheyfoot. Spectacular but harmless. Andy felt a pang of guilt at what they had done to Johnny. They had made him confess things he wouldn't want anyone to know in front of hundreds of people with the one he least wanted to hear them standing right next to him. And then he had been made tongue-tied in a truly terrifying way. In fact, they had humiliated him.

Andy watched road signs, shops signs, advertisements, slip by as the coach neared home. What must it be like not to be able to read them? Especially when you could before. It didn't bear thinking about. Nearly as bad as being blind or landing on another planet. He whispered to Dilip. 'Johnny's forgotten how to read.'

'He's lucky,' said Dilip. 'If it happened to me I'd have forgotten how to read in two languages.'

Without considering what Dilip meant, Andy's hands closed over the boots. Let Johnny read again, he thought.

A voice in his mind, very clearly, said, *He'll read again tomorrow*.

The dangleboots, alarmingly, were answering back.

He tried again. Why not now?

Tomorrow was the answer.

Andy left the dangleboots alone. This would have to be thought about.

They were back. Andy, avoiding the eyes of Len Symes, Mr Wheyfoot and Johnny, tore off home as fast as he could.

Back in the theatre the producer called an emergency meeting to sort out what had happened. The cast unanimously agreed that, for the rest of the run, audience participation was *out*. Gus Rentgarden was asked to come up with a new scene to start the second half before the next performance.

The man with leathery skin and the dark-eyed woman were packing up their stall in the deserted market place.

'Well, he didn't come today,' said the woman.

'He will,' said the man. 'He will.'

Doubting

On his way home, Andy promised himself a good think about the dangleboots. But before he had a chance, his father came back from work and before the evening meal Andy heard a row developing in the next room.

'I said we couldn't afford £3.'

'I'm not having him left behind when the others go.'

'Waste of time talking to you.'

'And to you. I can't reason with you.'

Not for the first time since Dad came back Andy saw things were not as rosy as he would have liked. But by the time they sat at the table a truce seemed to have been declared.

'What was it like, then?' said Mum.

'Great,' said Andy. 'Me and Johnny went up on stage. We were wizards.'

'See what I mean?' said Dad. 'They can't even afford enough actors to do their own play. It's much better watching the telly.'

So they weren't going to argue openly in front of him. That was a blessing. He went upstairs to think about the dangleboots.

One thing was clear. They were very powerful. To

bring Len Symes and Mr Wheyfoot on the stage must have taken real turbocharged magic. And those two deserved the neat revenges played on them. But Johnny was a different matter. What the dangleboots had done to him was surely cruel. He'd been really scared at suddenly finding he couldn't read. And telling a vast audience secrets he wouldn't want anyone to know about. He'll think he's going round the twist, thought Andy.

Andy took no pleasure in finding Johnny was afraid of him. He thought that after all he preferred the old relationship. At least he knew where he stood.

And there was something else. The dangleboots were changing. They seemed to be getting stronger. At first they didn't give themselves away. But in the theatre they'd kicked as if there were real feet in them. That was very worrying. So was the fact that *they had answered him back*.

He lay on his back looking at the ceiling. For the first time in his life he felt sorry for Johnny. The dangleboots had done all he wanted. And he wished they hadn't.

Dangleboots and the reluctant goalkeepers

Dilip hadn't been at Costers Park School very long. His parents had bought the grocer's shop just round the corner from Andy's house when the Chippendales sold up and retired earlier that year.

Andy liked Dilip. They sat next to each other at school and talked a lot outside it, wandering round the playgrounds and field when Johnny Caistor had other things to do than torment Andy. Often they walked home together. The shop was reached before the turn-off into Andy's road. Sometimes Andy went inside — once or twice to buy something, other times just to be greeted by Mr Lal or a relation sitting behind the checkout. If Mr or Mrs Lal was there, Andy usually found a Mars Bar or a packet of chickpeas put into his hand as he left.

Dilip was quiet and didn't take much interest, for example, in football. So Johnny Caistor, in turn, didn't take much notice of him. Being friendly with Dilip was, for Andy, like a rest cure.

For some time after the theatre visit, Johnny Caistor seemed just as he had been before. The next morning he could obviously read again. He never talked about what had happened on the stage and nobody else did either. Certainly not Andy. But the only difference was that Johnny left Andy alone. This was good. And Karen didn't shift her attentions to Andy. This was better.

So life went on quietly at school. The team — Andy sometimes in, sometimes out, Johnny Caistor ever-present — progressed well in the schools' district league and Cranbourne Road were the only serious rivals to winning it. Dilip sometimes came to watch but never really showed any interest.

At home, the going was rougher. Andy knew the rows were getting worse, the silences more oppressive. Sometimes, as he lay in bed and listened to indistinct raised voices, he thought: Dad'll be off again: I know it.

The changing rooms were nearly rebuilt. If no other big contract came up, Dad would be paid off and unemployed again. Surely the dangleboots couldn't be expected to keep Dad in work by systematically destroying the whole neighbourhood.

And the kick-abouts outside the lock-up garages were getting rarer too. Dad was preoccupied with something else.

What was it? Andy had a terrible clue. Voices through the wall were usually indistinct. But sometimes, when they were loud enough, he could hear them. And, one Friday night, his mother's voice was very clear.

'She's come here sniffing round after you, hasn't she? The bitch.'

When Andy woke up next morning his first thought was that above all else he'd like to kick a ball around with Dad outside the lock-up garages. But that wouldn't happen. Dad had gone out early, slamming the door behind him. Mum had retreated to the bedroom and didn't seem likely to come out. Things seemed as bad as they were before. Andy clutched the dangleboots desperately and muttered, 'Make it all right again.' The dangleboots stayed dead still, just lumps of black plastic.

He made his own breakfast, picked up the ball they played with outside the garages, and walked down the grey road. Frosty cold tanged his face. He came to the shop and entered. Warm, spicy air hit him and made him feel comfortable.

Mrs Lal was at the checkout. She guessed Andy was not there to buy anything.

'Stay here,' she said. 'I'll fetch him.'

Dilip appeared. He looked at Andy.

'What have you got that for?' he said.

'Got what?' said Andy.

'That ball,' said Dilip.

Andy looked at it.

'So I have,' he said.

He'd picked it up out of force of habit. He still wanted to kick a ball around. Dad wasn't available. Dilip was. But Dilip never played football. So why shouldn't he try?

'I don't play football. I never have,' Dilip said, after Andy had done his best to explain.

'Oh, come on. Try it. Just for once,' said Andy and Dilip unwillingly followed him.

Andy was not the world's greatest player, but having a ball at his feet seemed somehow natural to him. Ever since he could walk he knew a ball was something to kick. It was plainly not the same for Dilip. He was tall, thin and graceful in his movements. But with the ball at his feet he was stiff and awkward.

WIZZ
RULE
OK
BILLY
GAZ

The ball spun off the end of his toe or hit his knee. Once he actually fell over it. Andy became impatient.

'You're hopeless,' he said.

'I told you I never played,' said Dilip.

'Go in goal,' said Andy in disgust and made Dilip stand in front of one of the up-and-under doors.

Moodily, Andy walked the ball away from Dilip. Fat lot of use this morning was turning out to be. With Dad there, they could do brilliant high-speed passing movements. Dad would shout, 'On my head, son,' and Andy would lob over a perfect centre which Dad would nod downwards like a bullet into an empty goal. And Andy could do the same. But with Dilip — nothing.

He turned suddenly and fired the ball with all the venom he could. It flew towards the top left corner of the garage door. Dilip effortlessly leaned sideways and caught it cleanly over his head.

Andy stared. Dilip rolled the ball back.

Without a word, Andy hit it again. This time it sped two inches along the ground towards the opposite side.

Dilip had moved the right way even before Andy knew that was where the ball would go. On one knee, he collected the ball into his chest cleanly, then rose to his feet and rolled it back.

Andy still said nothing but belted it back straight at Dilip, in line with his stomach.

Once again, Dilip was perfectly behind the ball, caught it effortlessly and rolled it back.

Now Andy did speak.

'You're brilliant,' he said.

And he was. High, low, to right, to left, Dilip stopped

them all. Once he dived full length on the pitted concrete and jumped up without a scratch when Andy expected to see his knees grazed and bleeding.

'I know how to fall,' said Dilip. 'I used to do gymnastics.'

'You make Leggy Bowser look like a tree trunk,' said Andy. 'You'll have to be in the school team.'

'I don't want to be,' said Dilip simply.

All weekend, though, Andy couldn't get the thought out of his mind. Leggy Bowser was all right for much of the time. But he could make some pretty stupid mistakes as well. And no one else was any good at all. Besides, Leggy was a big mate of Johnny Caistor.

On Monday, Andy told Johnny what he thought. Dilip was there, looking bashful.

'I tell you, he's brilliant,' said Andy.

'He can't be,' said Johnny.

'He's *much* better than Leggy.'

'I don't believe it,' said Johnny.

'Don't listen to Andy,' said Dilip. 'I don't want to play in goal.'

'There you are, then,' said Johnny.

'It would be a terrible waste,' said Andy. 'No one could score against us if Dilip played.'

It showed just how much things had changed that Johnny didn't now call Andy a prat, wally or witless herbert. Instead, with the air of one lecturing a mental defective, he said, 'He can't be any good because they don't play football where he comes from.'

'What does that matter?' said Andy.

Johnny went on with his usual air of possessing all the knowledge known to the human race.

'They're all right at cricket. They can beat us, anyway. And they're brilliant at hockey - no one can come near them for that. But they *don't play football*.'

'I've never played hockey in my life,' said Dilip.

'Anyway,' said Johnny, turning to him. 'What part do you come from?'

'Luton,' said Dilip.

That finished the conversation. Andy felt he had a problem. He had discovered a brilliant goalkeeper nobody believed in and who didn't want to play anyway.

Why worry, he thought. I've got the dangleboots. While I have them, anything I want to happen it'll happen. I only have to wait.

The idea came to him when he was still in bed that night. A shoot-out. That's what they wanted. A penalty shoot-out. He'd seen them on television in the World Cup. It might not be very fair to settle whole games like that. But they were dead exciting. And they'd certainly sort out who was any good in goal.

He worked it all out. So that no one could say either Dilip or Leggy had it too easy, Johnny would have five penalty kicks at Dilip, Andy five at Leggy. Andy had to admit to himself that, Johnny being who he was, Dilip would have a harder time of it than Leggy would.

But that would make it better. And it might also make Johnny agree to the idea.

It didn't. Not at first. Johnny was scornful.

'How do you think you're going to get Leggy to say he'll do this? He'll know he's playing for his place.'

'If you think he's so good, there's no problem,' said Andy.

'What's that got to do with it?' said Johnny.

'He'll do it if you tell him to,' said Andy. 'Leggy's soft. He does anything you tell him.'

Johnny didn't answer, but wandered off. Presumably to find Leggy and tell him. On his own, Andy marvelled. Only a few weeks ago and that conversation could never have happened.

He then went off to persuade Dilip.

The shoot-out was arranged for the dinner-hour. Word spread and quite a crowd turned up to watch it. Mr Conway, looking through the staffroom window, saw kids gathering and thought he'd better see what was happening for himself.

Johnny had changed into his full kit. He couldn't bear to walk on to a football pitch without looking the part. He'd made Leggy change as well and he stood between the posts in his green jersey red-faced, portly and not looking very athletic. Andy had put his boots on while Dilip, looking as if he'd rather not be there, stood dazed in his trainers.

All this Mr Conway saw, and wondered what his charges were up to now.

Andy and Johnny tossed up. Johnny won and made Andy shoot at Leggy first.

The dangleboots in Andy's pocket stayed absolutely still.

Andy put the ball on the penalty spot and took six paces backwards.

'Wait a minute,' Leggy shouted and picked his nose. Then he crouched, arms slightly outstretched, waiting.

Andy ran up. He stumbled slightly and topped the

ball with the toe end of his boot. It skidded along the ground slowly to Leggy's left. Leggy made as if to give a furious arching dive, tripped over his own boots and sat down hard on the goal line. The ball rolled like a giant marble into the corner of the net.

'You dipstick, Leggy,' shouted Johnny.

His turn. The ball was on the penalty spot. Dilip stood on the goal line, arms by his sides. Johnny strode up and shot, low, hard and to Dilip's right. Dilip fell and clutched the ball firmly to his chest.

'Fluke,' shouted Johnny and Mr Conway started to take more interest.

Andy's next shot was very hard and straight at Leggy. It hit him in the stomach, knocked him backwards and was over the line before he could clutch at it. Johnny's next shot, high and to the left, was tipped over the bar by the leaping Dilip.

As Andy ran up to take his third, Leggy again shouted, 'Wait a minute,' and bent down to tie a bootlace. Too late — while Leggy fumbled, Andy's shot whistled in, hit Leggy on top of the head, skidded off at a sharp angle and ended up in the net.

Leggy scrambled up.

'You'll have to take that one again,' he gasped.

'Don't bother,' called out Johnny.

Dilip was beaten by Johnny's third. But so would anyone else have been. Leggy tried to save Andy's fourth with his feet: by the time it hit the back of the net it was travelling twice as fast as it was when it left Andy's boot.

'You're not trying, Leggy,' shouted Johnny in disgust.

'I am,' said Leggy desperately. 'I am. Honest.'

The spring-heeled leap with which Dilip pushed Johnny's fourth shot round the post made up Mr Conway's mind. No time for sentiment. Leggy's reign between the posts was over. Especially after Andy's last penalty hit him on the nose and made it bleed.

No one should have been able to reach Johnny's fifth penalty. Dilip got a hand to it, though he couldn't keep it out of the net. He stood wringing his wrist and shouting to Johnny, 'Careful. That hurt.'

Mr Conway prepared to have a word with him.

Well, thought Andy at home that evening. It all happened like it should. Leggy was awful, Dilip was great. Johnny's convinced and what's more important, Mr Conway was there and saw for himself. So Dilip's in goal from now on and Leggy's out. Dilip doesn't seem too pleased. But he'll get used to the idea.

He looked at the dangleboots. What marvellous things to have. I only have to ask and they make things turn out right every time.

He half expected to hear another message from them in his mind. But there was nothing. They stayed quiet and lifeless.

Andy put this down to the fact that they didn't have to exert themselves today. Not like back in the theatre. A problem like this they could probably solve in their sleep.

Andy woke up feeling rotten about Leggy. He knew too well what it felt like to be left out of teams. Guilt rose and hit him between the eyes. He'd done to someone else what he hated happening to himself.

'I've got to sort this out with Leggy,' he said aloud

before he got out of bed.

Yet Leggy seemed quite cool about it all. In fact — Andy noted with surprise when he went to him to offer sympathy — he was smiling all over his face.

'I'm not bothered,' he said. 'They can keep their rotten football team.'

'What?' Andy couldn't believe his ears.

'I hate it. I hate being in goal. Always have.'

'Why do it, then?'

'Because of that Johnny Caistor. He's always on at me. He thinks I'm good. I'm not. I'm useless. But I can't seem to get that into his head.'

'You have now,' said Andy.

'Nobody else wants to take my place because everybody thinks I'm a mate of Johnny's. Johnny's all right, but I just wish he hadn't got this thing about me being in goal. Anyway, I've shown him at last.'

Andy thought he detected a warning note in Leggy's voice.

'What do you mean?' he said.

Leggy ignored him.

'Do you know what it's like being in goal? No, you don't. You're too busy flailing round the field. Well, I'll tell you. It's horrible. It's like everybody's out to get you. You're kicked and pushed all the time. You never know whether to run out for the ball and get kicked on the head or stay back and get knocked into the net. As soon as you think you've got the ball some twerp on your own side gets in your way and then blames you for mucking things up. Make one mistake and everybody's on at you. It's all right out on the field. If you miss a chance by shooting over the bar, everyone says, 'Unlucky, Dangleboots,' and 'keep plugging away' and all stuff like that. But if I miss the ball we're a goal down and everyone shouts 'You useless pillock, Leggy' and I tell you it all gets right up my nose. So Dilip's welcome to it.'

All this poured out in a rush as if Leggy had been waiting to say it for years. Andy wanted to wind the tape back a bit.

'What did you mean,' he demanded, 'when you said, "I've shown him at last?"'

'I've shown him I was useless,' said Leggy. 'By letting all your pathetic penalties in.'

'They weren't pathetic,' said Andy. 'They were great. Except the first.'

'Not even I'm so bad that I couldn't have saved the lot if I'd wanted to,' said Leggy. 'Not making it look too obvious, that was the difficult bit.'

'I don't believe you,' said Andy.

'Johnny's right about one thing,' said Leggy. 'You're not much good. Still, I've done you a favour. Five goals from five penalties against the former school goal keeper can't be bad, can it? It'll do a lot for your reputation. Cheers, Dangleboots.'

And he was off, leaving Andy with a lot to think about.

'Aren't you going to thank me?' said Andy to Dilip.

'I'm not sure I've got anything to thank you for,' said Dilip. 'What have you let me in for?'

And the dangleboots still never moved.

And the man and the woman in the market still waited patiently.

Worrying

What Leggy said worried Andy. If Leggy had *tried* to look hopeless, then this time the dangleboots couldn't have helped. After all, there hadn't, this time, been a twitch out of them. Not like in the theatre . . . Even so, what he wanted happened in the end.

That could only mean one thing. It was going to happen anyway. Dilip was better than Leggy; Leggy didn't want to stay in goal. Everything today had been inevitable. So that meant *the dangleboots only worked when, without them, what was wanted was impossible.*

A disturbing thought, that. It made Andy look differently at all his new achievements so far. Without the dangleboots he'd be back where he used to be. Without the dangleboots he was nothing. All the while he possessed them, he was living a lie. That was no way to carry on.

He ought to get rid of the dangleboots and go back to being the pathetic little wally he used to be. Quickly.

Dangleboots and the daring daylight snatch

The next week was very strange. In the old days, while Andy privately thought he was an unrecognised genius, everyone else thought he was a wally. Now Andy knew he was hopeless, everybody seemed to think he was some sort of leader of fashion. The result, for him, was dizzying. And it was all the fault of the dangleboots.

But in spite of what he'd vowed, he couldn't bring himself to throw them away. He stood over drain covers, poised to drop the dangleboots through the grating. He paused by the river, drawing his arm back to hurl them into the water. He stopped by a stationary lorry and wondered whether to send them on a one-way journey to Macclesfield. Always he stopped short of actually doing it and walked on. No, he wasn't ready to rid himself of the dangleboots for a while yet.

Andy often wondered what his mother had meant that Friday night when she had said to her husband, 'She's come here sniffing round after you, hasn't she? The bitch.' Who was this *she*? And why did she sniff? Andy had a vision of a huge Alsation — female — padding round and round the house, nostrils wrinkling, all night. Perhaps that's why Dad slammed his way out of the house first thing every morning, to chase the creature away.

And perhaps not. Wishful thinking. Deep down, Andy knew the score. This was serious. And when Dad left the house so early, he didn't go to work. He didn't have any work to go to any more. All he wanted now was to stay out of the way. The house was as cold and uncomfortable as it used to be before Dad came back. Mum was as bitter now as she had been then. Sometimes she talked about it — *at* Andy rather than *to* him.

'I must have been mad, ever wanting him to come back here. If he goes this time, he can stay out for good. If he's got other fish to fry, that's his business, not mine any more.'

But Dad kept coming back. And now he never shouted. He was silent, miserable, his eyes dark and haunted. He sat moodily by the empty fireplace or stared sightlessly at the television.

'You're seeing her. I know it,' Mum would say.

'I'm not. Can't you believe me, woman?'

'Don't kid me. You're going to be easily caught.'

What had Mum said? Who was going to catch Dad easily? Was he in trouble with the police? Andy's heart sank.

'I've not been near her since.'

'I know you can't wait to get back to her. Well, you can for all I care. She's got her claws into you and she won't let you go.'

This would be the cue for Dad to rise to his feet and stalk outside, not to be seen again by Andy that night.

'Let him go,' Mum would say. *At* Andy again, not *to* him.

Those would be the last words spoken that

evening. In bed, Andy did what he had done when the dangleboots came his way and the Cranbourne Road game loomed. He closed the little boots into his hand and thought. I wish it could be like it was when Dad came back.

The boots stayed cold and lifeless in his grip.

They were all his mates now — Johnny, Dilip, Leggy and Karen. He was part of the inner ring, the elite. It was a pity he couldn't enjoy it. It wasn't nice to be there on false pretences. While the chatter swirled round him he went back into his shell.

And worse. He began to think he was being watched. It started on the walk to school the morning after the first sniffing conversation. Every morning the feeling seemed a little stronger. To and from school, eyes were following him. He looked behind him. Nothing. He peered forwards. Nothing. And at night, the idea that some huge Alsatian was outside the house — prowling, sniffing, watching — took hold of his dreams and marked out each morning as troubled and fearful.

He must be imagining things. That's what he managed to make himself think by the end of the day. The dangleboots were driving him mad. Nobody should meddle with unearthly powers like that. Yes, that must be it. He really would have to get rid of them.

That evening he leaned over the parapet of the railway bridge and tried to drop them into a coal truck in a freight train passing underneath. It would be a fitting end to the dangleboots if they perished for ever in the furnaces of a power station.

Once again he couldn't do it. The dangleboots ended up in their usual place — the pocket of his bomber jacket. Andy shuffled despondently back to his unwelcoming home.

Next day the hallucination was there again. As he walked on, loud talk going on all round him, eyes bored into the back of his neck. He felt them like laser beams. This was terrible; he really was going round the twist.

He turned round slowly.

'What's up, Dangleboots?' said Leggy.

'Nothing,' said Andy.

But there was something up. He wasn't imagining things after all. He was being watched.

A man and a woman, standing by a car. The car was a big Mercedes estate which had seen better days. So, it seemed, had the man and woman. The car was parked at the end of a small close of houses which Karen said was just like Brookside on TV. But it was not parked in the way anyone who lived there would leave his car — it was rather poised at the junction with the main road as if ready to make a quick getaway. Andy looked at all three — man, woman, car — and fixed the sight in his mind.

The woman leaned nonchalantly, one hand on the bonnet of the car, feet on the grass verge. The man stood by the driver's door like a chauffeur ready to admit his important passenger. The woman wore a cherry-red trouser suit. She was tall, with long, yellow, impossibly shiny hair curling down over her shoulders. Her face was thin with high cheekbones; her lipstick was the same cherry red as her trouser suit. Even from that distance Andy knew she was trying to appear a lot younger than she really was. The man looked half her height and four times her width. He was almost globular; a football with limbs and head. His black hair hung lank and his white face — dead pale against the dark grey of his rumpled suit — sweated so that it almost sparkled in the weak light of the December morning. Both faces wore fixed smiles.

Andy turned and walked on.

'Who are they?' said Karen.

'Nothing to do with me,' said Andy.

'The blonde beanstalk and the human toad,' said Karen.

Toad and beanstalk. Who were they? Why were they dogging his footsteps like this?

The doings of the school day went over Andy's head like a great flood while he tried, without success, to work it out.

They were still there on the way home.

The woman spoke as he passed.

'It's Andy, isn't it? Hullo, Andy.'

Andy pushed past. They were near Dilip's shop.

'Coming in, Dangleboots?' said Dilip. With relief, Andy followed him.

They were there next morning as well: standing in the same poses, car in the same place as if they had been rooted to the spot all night.

This time the human toad spoke as the five pushed past. He stepped into their path and oozed a treacly voice down Andy's ear.

'Ullo, sonny,' he said.

They all started running.

And again, coming home. This time the couple barred

the way by standing in the middle of the pavement.

'They're after you, Dangleboots,' said Johnny.

So they formed a sort of square rugby scrum: Karen, Johnny, Dilip and Leggy at each corner, Andy protected in the middle. Like a living cannonball they burst through the human barrier and didn't split up until they were outside Dilip's shop.

'Do you think they've taken the hint?' said Leggy.

It looked as if they had. Next day was Friday: the car and couple were gone.

'We've seen them off,' said Johnny.

Andy was pleased. But really they were the least of his worries. Last night the shouting had echoed and rolled round the house and into his stopped-up ears as he lay in bed. Then the door slammed so as to shake the foundations.

Next morning, Dad wasn't there. And the dangleboots had done nothing to help.

Just after break the school secretary entered Andy's classroom and whispered to Miss Brent. They both looked at Andy.

'There's a telephone message for you, Andy,' said Miss Brent. 'You're to go home as quickly as you can.'

Dumbly, Andy rose and the rest of the class watched him as he blundered out of the room.

He ran blindly out of the school gates, not knowing that the Head was making arrangements to have him driven home. There seemed to be a great void at the pit of his stomach and tears pricked the back of his eyes.

He was certain what he was going to find. Dad gone:

for good this time. Perhaps he had now been easily caught by the police. Mum in floods of grief, clinging to him for support. It seemed too much for him to bear.

Without looking where he was going, he collided with something soft. When he got his breath back he saw the pale watery eyes of the human toad.

'Do you want a lift back home?' said the human toad in his oily, flat voice. 'We can't have you out of breath when you reach your house, can we?'

He opened the rear door of the Mercedes. Andy stared at the luggage space.

'In you go,' said the human toad and pushed Andy so that he tipped over the back of the car and fell almost head first on to the floor. The human toad slammed the door and locked it. Then he sprang into the driver's seat and, without putting his safety belt on, roared off.

'This isn't the way to my house,' said Andy.

'I'm going the long way round to avoid the traffic,' said the human toad.

It seemed to Andy a very long way round indeed. Instead of turning left into his street, the human toad swung the Mercedes out on to the ring road.

'Where are we going?' shouted Andy in alarm.

'Don't worry. We'll be there soon,' said the human toad.

The Mercedes accelerated. They reached a roundabout with a big sign at the far exit saying *Motorway. To the South*. The Mercedes passed it and in a few minutes they were pounding down the motorway; the human toad moved up into top gear, cut across into the fast lane and exceeded the seventy speed limit by a big, big margin.

'Stop!' shrieked Andy.

'Can't stop on the motorway, son,' said the human toad.

Suddenly it dawned.

'I've been kidnapped,' Andy yelled.

'Of course you haven't,' said the human toad. 'We're just going for a ride. And you'll see your mum and dad at the end of it.'

Andy desperately looked through the window. He gestured and made faces at overtaken cars and lorries. The most reaction he got was waves and smiles from a party of old people in a coach. He started to thump the floor with his fists. Tired of that, he drummed his heels on the floor instead.

'That's no good,' said the human toad. 'The Jerries know how to make cars a bit too well for you to break up this one.'

Andy sat back on the carpet. What could he do? He was trapped. He was going to be murdered. Or held for ransom for a huge sum Mum and Dad could never afford. And he couldn't do anything about it.

Yes, he could. He'd got the dangleboots. They'd sort things out. They'd blow the engine up. Or tweak the steering so the human toad would swerve off the motorway and crash into a bridge. He'd write off the car, killing himself but leave Andy to walk unharmed from the wreckage.

Yes, the dangleboots would do it. He felt for the pocket of his bomber jacket to unzip it.

But the zip was undone.

And the dangleboots were gone.

When Johnny, Leggy, Dilip and Karen wandered slowly back home, they had no idea what had happened to Andy. And they weren't surprised to see no Mercedes, no blonde beanstalk, no human toad. Even so, they paused where the couple had stood.

'Let's go and see how Andy is,' said Karen.

'There's nothing wrong with him,' pointed out Johnny.

'It might be private,' said Dilip. 'Perhaps he won't want us.'

'There's nothing private about Dangleboots,' said Leggy.

'What are these?' said Karen.

She bent down and picked something up. The others gathered round to look at it.

A pair of tiny plastic football boots together with white laces.

'Who dropped the dangleboots, then?' said Leggy.

'Dangleboots did,' said Johnny, and the boys laughed; they thought he'd made a tremendous joke.

Because the extraordinary thing was that, though the dangleboots had changed Andy's life completely, nobody else had ever seen them. If the three boys there could have guessed what those little plastic objects had done to them they wouldn't have laughed quite so hard.

Only Karen didn't laugh. She examined the dangleboots carefully, said 'Dangleboots' thoughtfully, and then slipped them into a pocket.

'I'm keeping these,' she said.

Then they went to Andy's house. They knocked on the door: looked through the windows: went round the back.

The house was deserted.

When he found the dangleboots were gone, Andy

gave up. He curled himself in a ball on the floor of the car and prepared for whatever fate had in store for him. He wasn't frightened; he wasn't shocked. He just felt that the best thing he could do was to go to sleep.

Fat chance with the exhaust noise beating away just under his ear. When he sat up, the grey motorway landscape made him feel wretched.

At last the human toad turned off the motorway, following signs to places Andy had never heard of. Eventually they turned into a small close of detached houses with garages. Andy saw the name *Beasley Court*. Where have I heard of that before? The question nagged at him. The car stopped outside.

'Here we are,' said the human toad. 'Come on out.'

In the fresh air, with his limbs straight again, Andy felt much better for a moment. But then the human toad opened the front door, pushed Andy inside and slammed it behind him. A door at the end of the hallway opened. The blonde beanstalk appeared. She looked at Andy and her jaw dropped. The she turned on the human toad.

'What on earth have you done?' she shrieked.

'It's the quickest way to get what you want,' said the human toad.

'You idiot,' screamed the beanstalk.

'Trust me,' said the human toad, quite calm in the face of the beanstalk's anger. 'I know what I'm doing. I'm straightening out the corners.'

'You'll have us both inside,' howled the beanstalk.

'Never,' said the human toad. 'Once is enough. I know what I'm doing.'

And then it clicked. Not 'you're going to be easily caught, but 'you're going to Beasley Court'. Mum knew all about this place. He began to understand a little more. He also felt glad. It meant Dad wasn't in trouble with the police.

The human toad led Andy upstairs. 'In here,' he said. 'The room's ready.'

He opened a bedroom door.

Andy gasped.

A large room with white walls, maroon carpet and a big picture window draped with light grey curtains, and, alarmingly, with steel bars across it. The bed, made of stripped pine, had a check duvet on it, catching the colours of the walls, carpet and curtains. The walls bore pop group and football posters. In opposite corners were wall-mounted loud-speakers and on a smart white melamine table was a mini hifi. Next to it was a micro computer. There were shelves of books and racks of records and tapes. In another corner, mounted on a small shelf, was a portable colour TV.

Andy looked at it all in disbelief.

'All yours,' said the human toad. 'Not a bad place to wait in, is it?'

'It's nothing to worry about,' said Leggy.

Karen still looked doubtful.

'He must have had to go home because someone's ill,' said Dilip. 'Perhaps the whole family had to travel to some dying relative.'

'Maybe his granny's ill,' said Johnny.

'Anyway, there's nothing we can do,' said Dilip.

Karen still said nothing. She saw, in the lamplight, black spots of oil on the drive that Mrs Matthews' old Mini had dripped for years. She looked through the front window and thought she saw a mess, with cushions thrown around and a chair upturned. She tiptoed round the back and, through the kitchen window, saw a table still uncleared from breakfast and heard when she listened carefully - a radio still playing. She remembered the story of the *Marie Celeste*.

Dilip must have read her thoughts.

'Well, perhaps they had to leave in a hurry,' he said.

'Nothing's the matter,' said Johnny. 'I'm going home.'

Karen had still not spoken when she entered her own house.

Andy sat on the new bed, surrounded by objects he had longed for all his life. He drew his knees up to his chin and clasped his hands round them. *Nothing* would make him touch any article provided by the human toad. Or that dreadful woman.

What was he here for? Why had they done this to him? It seemed hours since the human toad had said, 'You'll see your mum and dad at the end of it'. Well, where were they?

I've had enough of this, he thought suddenly. I'll make a dash for it. He tried to open the door. No use. It must be bolted from outside. He looked out of the window. But his view was spoilt by the steel bars. No getting out of there, then. In any case, the ground below looked too far away.

He sat back on the bed for a moment. Then he got up again and started shouting.

'Let me out! Let me out!'

He kept this up for five minutes.

At last an answering shout came from the human

toad.

'Belt up.'

Andy went back to the bed. If only he had the dangleboots with him. He could do something then: escape, bring destruction down on the heads of his kidnappers, summon the SAS with carbines and helicopters. He'd tried so hard to lose the dangleboots. And now, when he needed them most, they had lost him.

Perhaps they could still work even if he wasn't actually holding them. All right, he thought. This is going to take some effort. But I've got to try. He started to build them up in his mind's eye: very carefully he concentrated until they appeared in every detail. His head began to ache with the effort.

But at last he could see them, shiny, black, with the little white stripes, as if they were there in his hand. He made sure the image was fixed in his mind. And then he spoke out loud.

'All right, dangleboots. Do something. I don't care how you manage it, but get me out of here.'

The day was ending and the market was deserted. But the dark-eyed woman and the leathery-skinned man still stood behind their stall.

In the darkening gloom the man spoke.

'I fear something is going badly wrong.'

But the woman's dark eyes sparkled in the lamplight.

'No, my love. I think everything is going exactly right.'

Seeing

Over the last few weeks, Karen had come to like Andy more and more. She had watched him blossom from class twerp to Johnny's rival. And she couldn't forget how he spoke up for her against Mr Wheyfoot when Johnny never said a word. So now she worried about him. He and his family had vanished, leaving nothing but an untidy house, spots of oil on the drive - and a pair of dangleboots.

That *must* be a sign. The dangleboots marked where Dangleboots had disappeared. Johnny thought it was a joke; Karen thought it was an omen.

In her bedroom was a little dressing table with a mirror. Now, in the evening when all was dark outside, she sat at it, thinking. The dangleboots stood on the table's smooth veneered surface. Karen stared at her reflection in the mirror as if looking into her own grey eyes would tell her where Andy was.

What can I do? Something is wrong: I feel it in my bones. But I don't know. And nobody else seems worried. It might only stir up trouble if I go to the police. What can I do?

She looked at the dangleboots.

Are you a sign? Do you know something I don't? If you do, I wish you could tell me.

A cold wind blew outside. Karen stood up to choose a cassette to play. Now she had her back to the dressing table. All at once, behind her, came a noise 'tap-tap-clickety-tap'. She turned. Just in time to see a movement. The left dangleboot hitting the top of the dressing table as if a tiny foot inside it had stamped. Fascinated, she bent down to look closely at the little black objects. And, as if they had decided to put a show on for her, the dangleboots began to dance; 'clickety - clickety - tap - tap - click' as if on the feet of an eighteen-inch high midget who ought to be in films.

Gingerly, she put out her hand to them. They kicked her with a force which she quite liked. Then, to her surprise, they hopped into her outstretched hand and stopped.

How surprising to her that she didn't feel frightened. Instead, 'I knew you were a sign,' she breathed. 'I wish I knew how to understand you.'

Still holding the dangleboots, she stared on into the mirror, at her round face with its snub nose, grey eyes and mousey-brown hair. And her reflection faded, clouds swirled around the glass of her mirror and cleared to show a room she had never seen before.

A room such as Karen had always dreamed of. The maroon, white and grey colour scheme looked so restful, the bed with its brand new duvet looked so comfortable, the hifi, TV and computer so inviting and the books on the shelves so bright and intriguing that it was some time before she realised someone was in the room.

A small figure sat at the modern white desk, head bowed and resting on the desk top, arms wrapped round it, a picture of misery.

She knew at once who it was. When the door started to open, the figure straightened up. Andy. She looked at the boots.

'Well, thank you for letting me see he's all right,' she said out loud. 'If he's ended up in a place like that, then lucky old Andy.'

Full of envy, she watched. Why was he so fed up? He should be over the moon.

The door opened fully. A man walked in. Karen stared. It was the human toad. That was her name for him and, now she looked at him again, she saw how right she was. He was *horrible*.

He carried a tray with a plate of baked beans on toast and a glass of orange. He set it down on the desk. Andy turned away. The man's mouth moved. No sound came through the mirror. But Andy put his hands over his ears. After a moment, the human toad said something which Karen could lip-read as 'Suit yourself' and walked out of the room, slamming the door behind him.

Then clouds scurried over the picture and Karen was peering at her own face once again.

She looked down at the amazing boots in her hand. 'I wish you could show me where that room is,' she said.

Because now she was sure. Andy was in big, big trouble.

Dangleboots and the day of deliverance

The baked beans congealed on the plate. Andy didn't care. Tired out, he crept into the bed, without putting on the brand new pair of cotton pyjamas laid out for him. Before he slept, he said aloud, 'I wish I knew how this was going to end. I wish it was all over. I wish I was out of it.'

As he drifted into sleep, the dangleboots appeared large in his first dream.

He woke suddenly. The room was in darkness. He lay quiet for a moment: then he heard the sound of a car drawing up outside and a slam of doors. Footsteps and voices came nearer. He got out of bed and looked out. He could see dimly by the light through an open downstairs window. Below him, about to enter the back door, were his father and the human toad. Each carried a large cardboard box which appeared to be heavy. They went inside the house: then reappeared for a moment. Obviously going back to the car at the front. Again they came into view. This time Dad carried a large box; the human toad two small ones. Again they disappeared inside: again they reappeared. The two stood together for a moment talking. Andy could see their lips move. They didn't seem angry with each other.

Tired suddenly, he scrambled back into bed. But before he could sleep he heard a loud, angry voice and recognised it with amazement. It was his mother's.

'Well, that just about puts the tin lid on it. You great fool. You twerp.'

Andy couldn't hear the muttered answer. But Mum wasn't finished.

'You haven't got the sense of a weevil. You shouldn't be let out, you shouldn't. What have I done to deserve being surrounded by men who are all idiots?'

Before he went to sleep, Andy had a nasty feeling Mum included him among the idiots.

When he woke again, day was here. So were a lot of difficult questions. What had all that been about? What were Mum and Dad doing here? Had they turned up at Beasley Court in search of him? Or had it simply been a very vivid dream? Or — and here he felt giddy — had the dangleboots done it again? Even though he didn't know where they were? The first time, they'd turned Saturday and Sunday around and everything had turned out right. And now he remembered — he'd wished for it, last thing before he went to sleep.

So where had he been last night? In this room or back in his own? He hadn't bothered to look.

But — and now he felt cold if that was a look of what was in store then things were very bad indeed. Dad and the human toad carting boxes around as if they were old friends: Mum screaming her head off at Dad worse than ever — what was the point of trying? Misery stretched forward for years ahead.

The door of the prison room opened. Andy braced himself for the human toad. But it wasn't. It was the blonde beanstalk. She carried a tray with cornflakes, a boiled egg, toast and coffee on it.

'Oh, Andy,' she breathed. 'Don't think too badly of us, please.'

Andy didn't answer.

'It was Grogan's idea to bring you here. Not mine. I told him it wouldn't work. But Grogan's so headstrong and, once he's made up his mind, nothing I can say will stop him.'

Andy still didn't answer.

'Don't you know who I am?' said the blonde beanstalk. 'I'm your Aunty Valma.'

'I haven't got an Aunty Valma,' said Andy.

'I'm not your *real* Aunty,' said the blonde beanstalk. 'But I'm surprised you've never heard of me. Oh, isn't that Alan a *naughty, naughty* boy?'

Andy thought she meant that someone his own age had been caught by the blonde beanstalk doing unspeakable things. But no. And anyway, the only person called Alan that Andy knew was his own father.

No, surely not . . .

'Yes,' said the blonde beanstalk. 'Didn't you know? Your father and I are *very* close. He stayed with me and looked after me for two whole years when your Uncle Grogan — my brother — had a little misunderstanding and had to go into prison.'

So *that* was where Dad was all that time before. With this weird woman. And probably here in

Beasley Court. And so the human toad had to be this Grogan.

'And then your father left me to go back to your mother. I was *so* sad. We were so happy together and I told him that you would be a big boy now and quite able to look after your mother. But he *would* go.'

And got knocked out for his pains, thought Andy.

'And then your Uncle Grogan came out of prison. When he found that naughty Alan had gone away again he was *so* cross. Of course, that was only because he wanted me to be happy. He said he would do terrible things to your father, like breaking his legs. But I told him not to. So I went to your town and saw your father to ask him to come back to me. But he wouldn't. I'm afraid he was *very* rude to me. And that made Grogan even crosser. Anyway, one day, Grogan said to me, 'How would it be if little Andy comes to live with us? We'll get a lovely room ready for him and then I'll collect him and then Alan will be only too pleased to live here and we can be one big happy family.' And that's what he's done.'

Andy could only think of one thing.

'What about Mum?' he said.

The blonde beanstalk laughed.

'Silly boy,' she said. 'I can't share Alan with anybody.'

She looked down at him.

'Here, eat your breakfast,' she said, plonked the tray down on the bed and left the room.

Andy was so hungry that he could now bring himself to eat food prepared in this house. As he chewed, he thought.

Yes, it explained everything. So this Valma was the one sniffing round that Mum hated so much. What a cow. Mum had got her number all right. Whatever was Dad thinking of?

His thoughts were interrupted by sudden shouts, screams and bangings as if a free fight was going on downstairs. He jumped out of bed and rushed to the door. This time, the blonde beanstalk hadn't bolted it from the outside. He crossed to the banisters at the top of the stairs and looked down.

At first sight, the hallway looked so crowded with angry, jostling people that he couldn't make any one face out. Then he saw that the human toad — he certainly wasn't going to call him Uncle Grogan — was there, waving his arms and yelling. The blonde beanstalk — and she was never going to be Aunty Valma either — had her hands over her ears and was screaming. Two men he hadn't seen before — just as ugly as the human toad but each about five times as large — stood silently, their arms folded. The sight of the fifth couldn't surprise him now — not after last night and then the talk with the blonde beanstalk.

It was his father. And he was shouting loudest of all.

Karen woke up with the same thought she had gone to sleep with. What can I do to help Andy?

Not much on my own, she decided. Who to go to for help? Not Johnny. She was going off him fast. Not Leggy. He was just Johnny's clone.

It had to be Dilip. He'd been Andy's mate longest — long before she had thought any more of Andy than Johnny did. The day of the theatre visit, that's when things had changed — that day of extraordinary happenings.

Extraordinary happenings. Like last night's? She

looked enquiringly at the dangleboots. They gave her no answer so she went round to the Lals' shop.

Dilip wasn't as surprised as she thought he would be about the dangleboots.

'I have heard of such things,' was all he said.

'So what do we do first?' said Karen.

'Go to where we last saw him,' said Dilip.

'And then to his home,' said Karen.

There was nothing to be seen where she had found the dangleboots. So they went to the house. Success at once.

Someone had returned. Mrs Matthews' Mini was parked in its usual place. So Karen knocked at the door. It was opened by Mrs Matthews herself, pale and with a tear-blotched face.

She and Karen both spoke at once.

'Have you seen Andy?'

'Come in, dear,' said Mrs Matthews when it was clear neither had.

'What about Dilip?' said Karen.

Mrs Matthews peered at him.

'Is he with you?' she said.

'Of course he is,' said Karen.

'All right, then,' Mrs Matthews said doubtfully and the two of them entered the house.

'You don't know what it's been like,' said Mrs Matthews. 'Andy's disappeared off the face of the earth. So has his father. If he's taken my Andy, I'll kill him.'

She burst into tears again. Karen didn't know what to do.

'Can I make a cup of tea?' she said. That's what her mother did when anybody was upset.

'I don't want tea,' wailed Mrs Matthews. 'I want

my Andy.'

'Where were you last night?' said Dilip.

'I thought Andy's father might have taken him away to that woman. I was so upset I couldn't stay in the house. So I went to my mother's for the night.'

And the tears started again.

They waited until this bout of crying stopped. Then Karen told Mrs Matthews about the couple with the Mercedes, ('It's her dreadful brother,' gasped Mrs Matthews), the message to school for Andy to come home ('That wasn't me,' said Mrs Matthews) and then how she had found the dangleboots. She produced them. Mrs Matthews wailed again.

'They're his. They're his. We must go to the police.'

The next bit was more difficult. How could she tell Mrs Matthews about the vision in the mirror? Dilip understood. But no adult would.

She had an inspiration.

'I think I'm clairvoyant,' she said. 'Like those mediums who help the police by dreaming about where dead bodies are.'

Mrs Matthews cried worse than ever. Karen thought she could have put that a bit better. When she had a chance, she went on.

'I had a really vivid dream last night. I dreamt Andy was in this bedroom with really nice, expensive gear all round him. But he looked so sad and fed up. Then this fat toad of a man came in with food. Andy wouldn't eat it. And that's it.'

Mrs Matthews stopped crying. She stood up. Her face had changed completely. Her eyes sparkled, her mouth set itself in a grim straight line.

'I know where he is,' she said. 'Beasley Court. I

knew Andy's father was a rat but I never thought he'd sink this low. Kidnapping his own son and taking him off to his fancy bit of goods and her mad brother.'

She rushed out towards the Mini.

'I'm off to get him back,' she shouted and yanked open the driver's door.

'What about us?' said Dilip.

'We're coming too,' said Karen.

'I don't want a lot of kids getting in the way,' said Mrs Matthews, buckling on her safety belt.

'But we're his friends,' said Dilip.

'We care about him,' said Karen.

Mrs Matthews looked at them standing together — Karen short and sturdy, Dilip tall and slim. Her mouth softened.

'Get in,' she said. 'Friends aren't so easy to come by nowadays.'

Half a minute later Mrs Matthews was urging all the Mini's 850ccs screechingly towards the motorway.

Dad seized the human toad by the lapels of his jacket and lifted him off the floor.

'Can't you understand, you thickhead? It's finished, *finished, finished*.'

The two large men unfolded their arms. Together they pulled Dad away from the human toad and threw him back against the wall. Then they returned to their places. The blonde beanstalk kept on screaming.

'No one upsets my sister,' said the human toad. 'She still fancies you, though God alone knows why. So you're going to be here with her and if your boy's got to be the sweetener to make you stay then so be it.'

'You're off your head,' croaked Dad. 'Prison's sent you round the twist.'

The two large men picked Dad up again and this time dumped him on the stairs. Now Dad, bruised though he was, turned on the blonde beanstalk.

'I told you I wasn't going to see you again. I must have been mad to take up with you in the first place.'

'How can you *say* that, Alan?' wailed the blonde beanstalk.

'I've learnt my lesson all right,' muttered Dad, feeling the side of his head where it had hit the banister.

'Not yet, you've not,' bellowed the human toad. 'You'll stay here. You and the boy. Try to leave and my mates here will carve you up so nobody will want to see you ever again.'

'I'll make you both happy, honestly, Alan,' the blonde beanstalk said in a high, wheedling voice. 'You'll see it our way soon. Time's a great healer.'

'It would have to be when my lads have had a go at him,' said the human toad.

There was a sudden furious banging on the front door.

'Get him upstairs before we see who it is,' said the human toad to the two minders. They hustled Dad upstairs and Andy just had time to dart into his room before Dad was pushed in to join him.

Dad looked at him without surprise.

'Sorry, son,' he said. 'What a mess I've made of everything.'

'Where have you been?' said Andy.

'I had to get away on my own yesterday,' said Dad. 'I had to think things out. When I came back in the evening the house was deserted. I'd gone out without my key. You and Mum had gone. I thought that was it, finished. I walked the streets all night. Then I thought the place to come was here, to settle the whole thing once and for all. So I caught the early train this morning, and here I am. What are you doing here?'

Andy told him.

'I'll kill that Grogan,' said Dad.

'Listen,' said Andy.

Whoever was at the front door was making a bigger noise even than the row which had just finished. This time there were high-pitched screeches, howls and the crash of falling furniture as if a full-scale fight was going on.

'It can't be,' said Dad. He listened. 'It is,' he said.

He tried the door. It was once again bolted from the outside.

'Come on, Andy,' he shouted. 'Get your shoulder to it.'

They took it in turns to shoulder-charge the door. At last, the bolt gave way and they looked down the stairs. The human toad and his minders stood watching the amazing sight. The blonde beanstalk was fighting another woman — slap, scratch, kick, all over the hall carpet.

'Oh, heck,' said Andy. 'It's Mum.'

The human toad had had enough.

'Get 'em apart,' he shouted to his minders.

With difficulty, they did so. Dad and Andy dashed back into the bedroom. The minders hustled Mum upstairs and pushed her in with them. Then they shut the door and, for the first time, noticed the broken bolt.

'You don't know your own strength, Garfield,'

said one.

'Move this wooden chest across the door, Crawley,' said the other. 'That should keep them in.'

There was the sound of something heavy being moved: then footsteps going back downstairs.

'Thank God you're all right, Andy,' said Mum when she saw him. She looked none the worse for her fight. The human toad must have stopped it because she was winning. Then she realised her husband was in the room as well. Her mouth clamped shut and she looked away. A heavy quiet descended which soon Andy couldn't stand.

'Look, Mum,' he said. 'It's not like you think. Dad came here to get rid of those people. And I was kidnapped. We've all got to stick together.'

'I don't believe you,' said Mum.

'It's true,' groaned Dad.

'We've got to escape,' said Andy.

Mum and Dad didn't take any notice. They were obviously settling down for what promised to be the biggest row of even their stormy careers together.

Karen and Dilip had watched fascinated as Mrs. Matthews hammered on the door, shouted 'That's her', as soon as it was opened and then set about the blonde beanstalk as if the world championship was at stake. Before the door was slammed in their faces by some huge gorilla in a grey suit they were sure they'd seen Andy on the stairs. And then they were shut out, alone in the unkempt garden of a strange house in a strange town.

'Now what?' said Dilip.

They looked helplessly round. Karen produced the dangleboots.

'If these things are so clever, they should be able to help us,' she said.

But they stayed lifeless in her hand.

'We'd better split up and explore the place,' said Dilip.

'You're a slob and a wimp,' shrieked Mum.

'I've done a few wrong things in my time,' said Dad. 'But I swear this time I was trying to make it up to you. I'm a reformed character.'

'You? You'll never change.'

'I came here to finish with this lot once and for all.'

'I don't believe you,' said Mum.

Andy wanted to believe. But, in spite of what he'd said to Mum, he couldn't. He'd seen into the future and Dad and the human toad were still mates.

'You're wrong about me,' yelled Dad.

'You're a weak-kneed idiot,' screamed Mum.

'And you're a nasty-minded hag,' bellowed Dad.

When Dad had come back before, Andy had thought adults were past understanding. Now he changed his mind. They weren't *worth* understanding. He fiddled with the window trying to find a way of getting out. And he was becoming more and more angry. At last he couldn't stand it any longer. He turned and faced them.

'SHUT UP,' he shouted at the top of his voice.

They stopped arguing and looked at him.

'I've listened to you fighting each other all my life,' he said. His heart was beating fast: he'd never say this again and he had to get it right first time. 'I'm fed up with it. I'd rather live on my own than put up with you two any more.'

'Now you've done it,' said Dad to Mum.

'It's both of you,' said Andy. He'd seen the future. He didn't care what he said. They'd never change.

'You make me puke,' he continued.

'But Andy . . .' Mum began.

'If we could get these bars off and you stopped thinking about yourselves,' said Andy, 'we could all escape from here.'

'What did you find?' said Karen.

'Not a lot,' said Dilip. 'That car of theirs is parked outside the garage. It can't get in because the garage is full of boxes.'

'What sort of boxes?' said Karen.

'There's all electrical goods in them. Videos, music centres, TVs, computers. I can read the labels through the window.'

'I bet the human toad pinched them all,' said Karen.

'What did you see, then?' said Dilip.

'I haven't seen anything. But I've heard something. A lot of shouting. And then Andy yelling, 'Shut up'. You could hear it a mile off. It came from that window up there.'

She pointed up to it and even as she did so, Andy's face could be seen looking through the glass.

'There's Karen and Dilip.' At last a shock that was pleasant.

'I know,' said Mum. 'They came with me.'

'Why didn't you say so?' demanded Andy.

Mum and Dad at least had the grace to look ashamed.

'If we could get these bars off . . .' Andy said again.

Mum looked scornfully at Dad.

'You're supposed to be the great handyman,' she

said. 'Surely you've got a screwdriver on you.'

Dad felt in his pockets.

'As a matter of fact, I have,' he said.

Andy noticed that Mum actually looked quite annoyed at this.

The bars were unscrewed in two minutes. Andy opened the window and called down to where Karen and Dilip stood below.

'Brilliant,' he said.

'I've got your little magic boots here,' said Karen. 'I can hardly hold them.'

She held the dangleboots up. They were capering in the air like an invisible country dance team that had taken up hang gliding.

'They brought us here,' she said.

'They're obviously pleased to see you,' said Dilip.

'Come on down,' said Karen.

Mum looked out.

'I'm not jumping that far,' she said.

'We can make a rope with the bedclothes,' said Dad excitedly. Finding the screwdriver and removing the bars had cheered him up a lot. 'I've always wanted to do that, ever since I was a little boy.'

They did so, tied it to the bedhead and in a minute or so were all on the ground with Karen and Dilip.

'Here are the boots,' said Karen and gave them to Andy.

'They've done a lot for you, haven't they?' said Dilip and Karen laughed. Suddenly Andy felt very happy. Here were two people who knew his secret and didn't think the worse of him. That's really what the dangleboots had done all the time — given him friends and reasons for them to respect him.

No time to think of that. There was a lot to be done.

'What do we do now?' he said.

'Back to the Mini,' said Dad. 'Your mum's the driver.'

'He can't even do that,' said Mum.

'Give it a rest,' said Dad. 'If you put your foot down we can get home before this lot wake up and we might be in a car chase up the motorway.'

'You think a Mini can get away from a Merc?' said Mum.

'It won't come to that,' said a voice. 'You're going nowhere.'

The human toad, the blonde beanstalk and Garfield and Crawley, the minders, stood in a row blocking their path. The men folded their arms and smirked. The blonde beanstalk shot soulful glances at Dad.

'I'm very discontented about all this,' said the human toad. 'Some of us don't seem to understand where our true interests lie.' He looked at Dad as he spoke.

Why should we worry? We've got the dangleboots on our side. That's what Andy thought. He felt them in his bomber jacket pocket. But it looked as if Dilip was right: they had indeed been dancing before because they were pleased to see him. Now, they were as dead as the day he'd first seen them hanging on the market stall.

Come on, dangleboots, he muttered to himself. *It's now we need you*.

Garfield twisted Dad's arm behind his back and bundled him into the back seat of the Mercedes. Crawley did the same to Mum. They tied their wrists together and slammed the doors.

The dangleboots didn't move. Come on, urged Andy. Then a voice came into his mind, just as it had when Johnny found he couldn't read.

We've done all we can for you. From now on, you're on your own.

There was only one thing for it.

'Run,' shouted Andy. 'Run as hard as you can.'

But where to? The enemy blocked the only way out to the front, between the garage and the house. The weedy, stony, untended garden was bounded by a wooden fence five feet tall that it would be hard to get over in a hurry.

So nobody ran. The human toad laughed: Garfield and Crawley smirked more than ever.

'You've had it now,' said Garfield.

Then someone did run. It was Dilip. He dashed for the fence twenty metres away at the far end of the garden.

He was about to vault over (Andy remembered Dilip used to do gymnastics) when the human toad spoke.

'You won't get anywhere that way, sonny. More gardens, more houses: we'll pick you up in no time.'

Dilip paused and looked back. The human toad spoke to Garfield and Crawley.

'Get him,' he said.

The two heavies lumbered forward.

Since he had discovered what a good goalkeeper he was, Dilip had taken the art very seriously. He'd played three times for the school already and not let one goal past him. And in practices he was always trying new things — especially those he saw on the television from the likes of Peter Shilton and Bruce Grobbelaar. What thrilled him most was when a goal keeper rushed out, timing it perfectly, dived at the feet of a forward, collected the ball and shielded both it and himself with his back from kicks from flying feet. That took both talent and nerve and was what he practised most.

So when he saw Garfield and Crawley running towards him, he thought: time for another practice.

How can I stop them? They'll murder Dilip. Andy watched frantically as if it was an awful slow motion film. Twice he'd stopped people in their tracks since he'd had the dangleboots; each time with deadly striking. He'd laid out his father: he'd clobbered old Len Symes. With a ball at his feet and when the force was with him it seemed he could hit anybody.

But now, when he needed one, he hadn't got a ball at his feet. Still, there were stones on the ground in this dishevelled dump. He turned as he had on the day the ball came over from the left, he had hit it sweetly with his right foot and sent Dad into hospital.

Dilip imagined that the ball was coming over from the left and Garfield would hit it on the volley if he didn't smother it first. His eyes fixed on something that wasn't there, he galloped out, dived on it keeping his body between ball and oncoming player and allowed Garfield to trip harmlessly over him.

Andy's foot caught the large pebble perfectly. It flew, rising to knee height, like a dart destined for treble twenty. Just as Crawley was about to join Garfield, the pebble hit him plumb on the moving joint of his left knee.

As Garfield sprawled forward, losing his balance, Crawley's scream of pain could be heard far away from Beasley Court. They fell towards each other. The thud as their heads collided made Andy and Dilip wince.

Garfield and Crawley were out cold and would take no further part in the game.

Everybody stared. Then Andy and Dilip ran to each other, arms punching the air, and hugged as though it was the winner at Wembley. The human toad looked nonplussed — just for a moment. Then he spoke.

'All right. I can do without those two wallies. It's time for us to be out of here.'

Andy then realised that all he and Dilip had done was cut themselves off from his parents. And the human toad had them trapped between him and the Mercedes estate, standing there with its tailgate open where the blonde beanstalk had been stowing cases and rugs.

'You think you're clever, don't you?' said the human toad. 'Well, I'm having the last laugh. I kidnapped you yesterday. Today, I'm kidnapping your parents. You won't know where they're going. When I've got them to myself, I'll soon make them both see sense. I'll leave you here to cool off and then my two mates can deal with you when they come round. You've made them look very silly. And besides, you've seen our little secret in the garage. They won't be very pleased with you.'

'You can't make us go with you,' shouted Mum. 'Do something, Alan.'

'Don't be daft, woman. What can I do?' muttered

Dad.

Andy thought he now had a pretty good idea why they would still be arguing in the future.

The human toad slammed the rear door and seated himself behind the steering wheel. The blonde beanstalk sat beside him. Mum and Dad slumped miserably on the back seat. The human toad started the engine: the exhaust burbled. The Mercedes purred out into the road.

Dilip and Andy looked at each other.

'Where's Karen?' said Dilip.

'No idea,' said Andy. 'Gone off home at the first sign of trouble probably.'

'What do we do now?' said Dilip.

They looked over at Garfield and Crawley. Both were still out cold.

'Ring the police?' suggested Dilip. 'We can tell them about the stuff in the garage.'

'That's no good. The toad will use Mum and Dad as hostages.'

No more than they deserve, Andy thought privately. But he wouldn't tell Dilip that. The police would only muck things up.

They stood in thought, eyes looking at the ground. So the quiet application of brakes and the 'burble-burble' of the Mercedes' engine didn't register for a second.

They looked up. The human toad had not driven away at all. He had merely gone a few yards down the road; then quietly reversed up the drive so now Andy and Dilip were trapped between car and garage door. There was no way out.

The human toad jumped out.

'See?' he said. 'You have to get up very early in the

morning to put one over on me. Well, I've got you now. I want you where I can keep an eye on you. Now we can all go for a ride.'

Although he looked like a punctured football with trousers on, the human toad was very strong. Andy and Dilip cowered together in the corner between garage and fence and lashed out when he approached them. But they couldn't stop him seizing their arms and — to their amazed horror — handcuffing them together. He pinched them out of the last cell he was in, thought Andy. He then caught each by the scruff of the neck and pushed them round to the side of the car. The blonde beanstalk leaned over and fiddled with the inside of the rear passenger door. Then the human toad opened it.

'I knew the baby-locks would have a use one day,' he said.

He pushed the two boys in so they were squashed up against Mum and Dad. Then he opened the glove-box, fished out a note book, tore a page out, wrote on it in large capital letters GET RID OF GOODS IN GARAGE PRONTO THEN MEET US YOU KNOW WHERE, gave it to the blonde beanstalk, said to her, 'Shove it in Garfield's breast pocket so he'll see it when he comes round,' sat back in his seat, fastened his safety belt, started the engine, switched on the cassette player so that Shirley Bassey's voice roared out of all four speakers and let his face assume an expression of quiet triumph.

The blonde beanstalk returned. The Mercedes moved smoothly out of the drive, out of Beasley Court and towards the open road.

The back seat of the Mercedes was very large. But

four people were too many for it — especially when each pair was tied together. Mum and Dad were silent: indeed, wouldn't look at each other. Andy and Dilip were creased up with discomfort.

They left the town behind. Soon they reached the motorway. The car turned the opposite way to home. Then it thrummed along the motorway, putting another mile between them and safety every forty seconds.

Now we're really in it, thought Andy. And the dangleboots have opted out — we're on our own.

Something pulled his ear.

'Stop it, Dilip,' he said. 'Leave my ear alone.'

'How can I touch your ear?' said Dilip. 'Have a bit of sense.'

Andy looked back. The luggage space had suitcases and rugs in it: to his horror a hand appeared from under a rug and moved to and fro like a snake coming out of a snake-charmer's basket.

'What's this 'ere?' said a muffled voice which Andy heard plainly over the outpouring of Shirley Bassey.

Then the rug moved again. A face appeared. Its owner put fingers to lips before Andy could shout out in delight.

It was Karen. She threw off the rug and Andy saw how she had hidden herself, crouched in a corner of the luggage compartment.

'I'm here to rescue you,' she whispered.

'You can't do that,' said Andy.

'Can't I, though,' she said and sat up. In her other hand was a wicked looking length of iron piping.

'That lot don't care what they leave around,' she said.

Mum and Dad turned round. Karen went through the same finger on lip routine to shut them up, then said, 'All four of you move around a bit as if you're trying to get comfortable so I can climb over the seat without them noticing.'

'We'll be squashed to death with you here,' said Andy.

'Listen,' said Karen. 'Do you *want* to be rescued?'

So they did as she said, under cover of the sound of 'Big Spender'. Soon she was wedged awkwardly between Mum and Dad and directly behind the human toad. She waited a moment, then lifted the iron piping, pushed it round the side of the driver's headrest and into the human toad's ear.

'Turn that tape off,' she shouted.

Without turning round, the human toad did so.

'I only did that to hear what you had to say,' he said. 'Don't think you're frightening me. I know that's not a gun.' Karen lifted the piping again, so it was poised over the human toad's head.

'I know it's not a gun as well,' she said calmly. 'But it wouldn't half make a dent in your thick head.'

'Put it away,' said the human toad. His eyes, they could see through the mirror, were fixed intently on Karen's reflection. 'Don't play games.'

'This isn't a game,' said Karen. 'You're going to drive us home.'

'No chance,' said the human toad and the Mercedes moved up to 1OOmph.

The blonde beanstalk nudged him.

'Slow down. You don't want to be nicked for speeding, not now.'

'If you don't drive us home, I'll smash this down on your head.'

'You wouldn't dare,' said the human toad. 'I'm driving. If you do that we'll all be dead.'

'*You* will be,' said Karen. '*We* won't. It's the front seat passengers who are in danger. Those in the back seat get out alive.'

'If you don't put that thing down, I'll test your theory out,' said the human toad. 'I'll drive into the crash barrier. Then we'll see who's safe. We've got belts on. You haven't.'

The other four in the back seat were too flabbergasted to check this amazing conversation which was being carried out with complete calmness on both sides.

'I'll count ten,' said the human toad. 'And if you haven't put that piping down by then I'll crash this car deliberately. Then we'll see who escapes. One.'

'Grogan,' screamed the blonde beanstalk. 'Stop it. You'll have us all killed.'

'Two,' said the human toad.

'You're off your rocker,' shouted Dad at Karen.

'Three,' said the human toad.

'You think of another way, then,' said Karen.

'Four,' said the human toad.

'You're wasting your time,' said Karen to him. 'I'll put it down at ten all right. I'll put it down square on your bald patch. We'll keep on the road because your sister will lean over and take the wheel when I've put you out for the count. She won't be able to stop herself doing it.'

'Rubbish,' said the human toad. 'Five.'

'And anyway, you won't crash your car when you've got to ten. You wouldn't even let the paintwork get scratched,' said Karen.

'Six,' said the human toad.

Karen's eyes were shining: the iron piping in her hand never wavered. Andy and Dilip watched her with absolute admiration. They'd been pretty pleased at the way they'd taken Garfield and Crawley out of the game. But this . . .

'Seven,' said the human toad.

'You may as well stop counting,' said Karen. 'I've scared you. You'll leave the motorway at the next exit and go up the other way.'

'Never,' said the human toad. 'Eight.'

'Am I right? Or are you? You don't know, do you?'

'Nine,' said the human toad.

Karen didn't flinch. They passed the one-mile sign for the next exit.

'You can leave the motorway here,' said Karen.

'Ten,' said the human toad.

'Crash us, then,' said Karen. 'Or I'll hit you.'

The human toad's hands showed white on the steering wheel. Beads of sweat appeared on his forehead. The silence in the car crackled. They seemed to be travelling through outer space with time stood still. Then the human toad switched on the left-hand indicators, came out of the fast lane and entered the slip road.

There was a collective sigh of relief in the back seat. The blonde beanstalk burst into tears and fumbled in her handbag for a tissue. The car circled the roundabout under the motorway, then joined the other carriageway.

'I'm not letting you off the hook,' said Karen. 'I've still got this piping held over your head. And I'll use it.'

The Mercedes was now hurtling in the opposite direction. Karen spoke to the blonde beanstalk.

'Untie Mr and Mrs Matthews,' she said.

The blonde beanstalk looked at the human toad, who nodded. Then she produced a pair of nail scissors from her handbag. Mum and Dad awkwardly manoeuvred themselves so they could present their joined wrists towards her and she cut through the string.

'Now the boys,' said Karen.

'Key in my pocket,' muttered the human toad.

The blonde beanstalk fumbled for a moment, produced it and in a few seconds Andy and Dilip were free as well.

Forty minutes later they were home. Freed passengers burst out of the car. The human toad and blonde beanstalk slumped miserably in the front seats.

Karen at last put down the iron piping. She stepped out of the car.

And fainted.

Inside the house Mum remembered something.

'I want my Mini back.'

'Get it back for her, Grogan,' said Dad. 'Or I'm off to the police.'

'Get knotted,' said Grogan. Now he was out of the car his spirits were reviving a little.

'Dial 999, Andy,' said Dad.

Andy went to the telephone: before he could dial, Dad spoke again.

'He'll do it, Grogan. Unless you ring up your two apes. If they've recovered yet. They can bring it back.'

'All right,' muttered the human toad.

'They haven't got the keys,' said Mum.

'That's never worried them before,' said Dad.

The human toad dialled, listened, then spoke. Garfield and Crawley had obviously come to.

'Change of plan,' he said. 'Bring the Mini here.'

Silence. Then the human toad turned round enquiringly.

'They haven't got the keys,' he said.

No one answered.

The human toad turned back to the phone.

'Do what you always do,' he said. 'And be quick.'

He slammed the phone down. He looked defeated.

'I want a word with you outside,' said Dad.

At night, when all was over, the Mini returned, Karen had recovered, she and Dilip were home and Andy was in bed, he woke.

It was dark. The sound of a car stopping, doors slamming and voices made him get out of bed.

This has happened before, he thought. And the feeling that it had all happened before made him suddenly certain that it had all happened before.

Of course. Unlike the first time, the dangleboots were making him live through a glimpse of the future twice. So he knew he was going to see Dad and the human toad humping boxes and knew he was going to hear Mum screaming at Dad.

And he was right. Just the same.

But *why* did Dad and the human toad seem friendly? And *why* was Mum screaming? All in all, Dad had done pretty well the day before.

It was a puzzle.

And then he slept.

He woke again next morning. For a ghastly moment

he thought he was back in the prison bedroom. In front of him were the same TV, the same hifi and the same speakers. He sat up in bed and stared at them in horror.

It was 7.30 a.m. on Sunday morning. Dad stood next to his bed, looking down on him and smiling.

'What are those things doing here?' demanded Andy.

'I thought it was the least that Grogan could do,' said Dad. 'He's finished. The police are after him. He'll go back inside. We won't hear any more from him. I've got too much on him. And Valma will soon find someone else to leech off.'

'But how did that lot get here?'

'I thought you deserved something out of all this mess,' said Dad. 'So on Saturday I tried to get Grogan to give me the goods he'd put in the room he shut you in. I told him that if he didn't go back and get them and have them back here before ten o'clock last night I'd put the police straight on to him. Well, friend Grogan's changed a lot - so he did. And I made sure it was all good stuff. So here you are, Andy. It's all yours.'

The bedroom door burst open. Mum stood there, very angry.

'I heard that,' she said.

'Oh, go away, woman,' said Dad. 'We had all this out last night.'

Mum spoke directly to Andy.

'Your father is a *fool*,' she said. 'You'd have thought he'd have had enough of all this yesterday. But no, he can't keep his sticky little fingers out of things.'

She turned to her husband. 'That's stolen goods,'

she shrieked. 'You're *worse* than Grogan. And twice as stupid.'

'The kid deserves something out of all this,' said Dad.

'I don't know why I bother,' said Mum. 'To think that once I *wanted* you back.'

Dad looked directly at Andy.

'I did this for you,' he said.

'You'll end up in prison,' said Mum.

Andy felt a great tug in his heart. Marvellous things were his. What he'd always wanted. But . . . though it hurt him, he had to say it.

'I don't want them, Dad.'

'What do you mean?''

'I couldn't use them. They come from *them*. *They've* touched them. They tried to bribe me with them. I can't have them in my room.'

'But that's all finished, Andy,' said Dad.

'I don't care. I don't want them. They're stolen. And besides,' — here was something he felt very sure of — 'I don't deserve them.'

Dad's face fell.

'That's not how it looks to me,' he said. 'But I'll respect what you say. This gear won't be here when you come home from school.'

And suddenly, Mum smiled at Dad — smiled just as she had on that other day when he had eaten scrambled egg and his swollen face was yellow and black. Dad cleared his throat and clumsily, almost shyly, reached out to his wife.

Andy looked at them both. It might, he thought, it might, it just *might* be all right in this house again.

Rejecting, rejoicing, returning

Andy met them all on the way to school on Monday. His friends. Johnny and Leggy were told about everything: their envy of great doings was pleasing to watch. Dilip and Karen were full of it. And as he watched them and listened to them Andy thought: My friends. My *real* friends. They stuck by me.

And the dangleboots brought them to me. *That's* what they really did.

He clutched the dangleboots as he walked. What did they mean to him now? Did he depend on them too much? Yes, he did. After the business of Dilip, Leggy and the penalty shoot-out he'd wanted to get rid of them. They had told him too much about himself.

Just as well he hadn't. Where would he be now without them? But that was the trouble. He was the sort of person things happened to. He never did anything for himself, never took a decision, never made his mind up. When he *tried* to be original he made an idiot of himself. Lately, the dangleboots had done it all.

But that was wrong. On Saturday, they both had deserted him. And yet they had all come through. By their own efforts. And, what had he done yesterday?

He *had* made a decision. A big one. He'd been offered things he really wanted and turned them down. And he knew he was right. *And* original. And it looked as though what he decided had brought Mum and Dad together.

All my life, and that's the very first time, thought Andy. I've made a decision and stuck to it. And it worked.

And I've stood on my own feet. What Dilip and I did to the two heavies on Saturday was great. I'm a striker where it counts. I *meant* to do it. And if it wasn't for the dangleboots I couldn't have done it.

But Karen. That was something else. She was superb. Dilip and I were nothing to her. She'll never need anything like the dangleboots. Ever. Not like me.

The dangleboots moved in his pocket. Once again, the voice spoke in his mind. *You couldn't get rid of us but now perhaps it's time for us to get rid of you.*

You're right, thought Andy. I can't go through life with you to prop me up. You've been good to me. But now I must do it on my own. We'll have to part company.

'Colds and 'flu this time of year,' said Mr Conway. 'They cut the squad in half. Leggy, you'll have to play. In midfield.'

'Great,' said Leggy. 'What I always wanted.'

A big game for Costers Park after school on Thursday. Who should it be against but Cranbourne Road again? But not on either school pitch. This time it would be under floodlights, on the all-weather pitch at the big new sports complex. And they'd all be in the team - Dilip in goal, Leggy drafted to the

midfield, Johnny and Andy two strikers.

When the time came and Andy ran out on to the pitch he saw among the spectators the casts of all his little dramas, appearing as if for the final curtain. Karen was there, shouting her head off like some American cheerleader. Mr Wheyfoot was there as guest of the Head on this big occasion for the school. Standing near them was Len Symes. But only because his nephew was playing for Cranbourne Road. And Mum and Dad were both there. Dad was already tuning his voice up. 'Come on, Andy. Keep hitting them and the goals will come. Get stuck in. You could have six.'

'We haven't even started yet,' said Johnny.

Miss Brent stood next to Mr Conway on the touchline. To Andy, the roll call was so complete that he even looked round for the human toad and the blonde beanstalk. But by now they had other things on their minds.

And then the game was on. For Costers Park, everything went right. Dilip, Leggy, Johnny and Andy played out of their skins. It was a hard, even game but at half-time Costers Park were 3-0 up. Striking and goalkeeping made the difference. Johnny scored the first two, Andy the third with a shot that left his boot sweetly and hit no one on the way. They gloried in their partnership. Leggy bustled round the field getting redder and sweating more and doing the work of three. Dilip was brilliant beyond his years. At half-time Mr Conway almost felt like crying with delight at his charges.

'Words fail me,' he said to them.

'I'll tell you what,' whooped Johnny, his arm

round Andy's shoulders. 'Second half we'll play 0-0-10.'

'Don't muck it up,' said Mr Conway.

They didn't. They didn't play 0-0-10 until the last five minutes when they were 5-0 up. Johnny had scored three, Andy two. And at the very last gasp word went round the team and they tried it. All ten bore down on the quaking Cranbourne Road goalkeeper. For a moment all was confusion. Then Andy struck. His second hat-trick for Costers Park School. And this time he had meant to do it.

'Well done, lads,' said Mr Conway.

'Good boys,' said Miss Brent.

'I see a remarkable amount of individual potential in your team,' said Mr Wheyfoot to the Head. 'Allied, of course, to superior all-round cohesiveness.'

'Not bad, I suppose,' said Len Symes grudgingly. And to his nephew, 'You were lucky to get none.'

Meanwhile, Karen was feeling resentful.

'Nobody comes to shout for us girls like this,' she said.

'It's a man's world. You'll find that out,' said Mrs Matthews.

'It had better change itself, then, hadn't it?' said Karen grimly.

'My voice has gone,' croaked Dad.

As they all went home, Andy thought: That's it then. Things are as good as they can be. They might get better; might get worse again. That's up to us now.

The dangleboots had done their job. He didn't need them any more.

*

Saturday morning. Andy strode through the market place, looking for the stall. As he drew nearer the crowds were fewer, quieter: the stalls became smaller, dowdier.

Yes, there they were, right at the far edge of the market. The same charms, Cornish Piskies, Joan the Wads, gonks, little dolls. And on the front of the stall, a nail stuck out with nothing hanging from it. Standing side by side, watching him, were the dark-eyed woman and the leathery-skinned man.

Andy faced them.

'I've brought the boots back,' he said.

'What have you found out?' said the woman.

'A lot,' said Andy.

'Was I right?' said the man.

'You were,' said Andy.

'Are you glad you bought them?' said the woman.

Andy thought.

'I think so,' he said.

'Only think?' said the man.

'No,' said Andy firmly. 'I know so. I needed them. They've done well for me.'

'We knew they would,' said the woman.

The man was counting out money. Andy looped the boots back over the nail. The man put his hand out: there was a pile of coins on his palm.

'80p,' he said. 'That was the price, wasn't it? You didn't buy them. You rented them for a while.'

There was nothing more to be said.

'Thank you. And goodbye,' said Andy.

He turned and walked away. Soon the man and woman lost sight of him as he melted into the crowd.

They stood together for a long time. Then the woman nudged the man. A girl of about eleven was approaching the stall. She looked almost fearfully at the couple and nearly turned away. But she came back, rummaged among the articles on the counter and finally picked up a small glass unicorn, clear but with coloured spirals which shimmered through its body. She looked at it carefully; wrinkled her snub nose and then looked at the couple with steady grey eyes.

'Like it then, dearie?' said the woman.

'It's all right,' said Karen.

The woman spoke again.

'What would you say if I told you . . .?'